The Inheritance

Pamela S. Thibodeaux

Now I commit you to God and to the word of his grace, which can build you up and give you an inheritance among all those who are sanctified.
~Acts 20:32

The Inheritance
By Pamela S Thibodeaux

Publisher/Distributor:
Temperance Publishing; an imprint of
Pamela S. Thibodeaux Enterprises, LLC
PO Box 324, Iowa, LA 70647

Cover Design: Get Covers

Published in the Unites States of America

Publishing History: First White Rose edition 2007 The Wild Rose Press
Second White Rose Edition 2017 Pelican Book Group
All Rights have Reverted to Author

Dedication

For Bryanna. My light, my life, my Angel Girl.

And Judy, my friend and critique partner. Your friendship, support, and constant challenging me to grow as a writer has blessed my life more than you'll ever know.

***Thank You*, Dear Reader.** I pray you've been as blessed as I have by your purchase of this book. If you've enjoyed **The Inheritance,** please write a positive review, and post it at online retailers and websites where readers gather and/or your social media platforms (FaceBook, Good Reads, BookBub, Twitter, etc).

Chapter One

"They say life begins at forty."

Caught somewhere between wakefulness and sleep, Rebecca Sinclair rolled over, pulled the covers up to her chin and wondered where that thought came from. "Boy is that ever far from the truth," she mumbled to whoever's voice had invaded her dreams. "If this year is anything like the last one, I might not make it."

Here she was, on the downhill side of thirty-nine and counting the hours with dread and fear of what the next year would bring.

So much had happened in one short year, beginning with the death of her husband. That day had started out like any other. An ordinary day in the ordinary life of Jim and Rebecca Sinclair. Only it ended far from ordinary when Jim's car skidded off the road into a ravine. Investigations later reported that a massive heart attack, and not the accident, had taken his life.

She still couldn't believe it, a heart attack. At forty-one, Jim had been the picture of health. He'd always taken excellent care of himself—ate right, exercised. Work hard, play hard, and live right had been his motto. And he'd done just that. Right up to the end.

Fighting back memories and tears, Rebecca tried desperately to snuggle in the too-cold bed and to concentrate on happier times when she'd looked forward to turning forty. *When I turn forty, my youngest will be eighteen and out of school, and I'll be through raising kids!*

How many times had she said that? Laughing and carefree, looking forward to the day. "Well, at least that much is true," she murmured.

The phone rang, jolting her out of her reverie. She picked up the receiver and was greeted with a chorus of "Happy Birthday" from her son. His warbled rendition made her giggle.

"Thank you, but doesn't all that Broadway training include singing lessons?"

Jeff laughed. "Yes, but the acting lessons allow— even encourage me—to do things out of the ordinary. Have you heard from Debbie?"

"Not yet. We still haven't gotten used to the time difference. Besides, I imagine she's pretty busy since school just started."

"Yeah, busy studying to be the greatest medical scientist of the twenty-first century," Jeff said, pride in his sister evident in his voice. "Finding cures for all the plagues of the twentieth century-diabetes, cancer, heart disease, and AIDS."

"If anyone can do it, Debbie can. So, what's on your agenda for the day?"

"More of the usual: classes, rehearsals, and work."

"Well, you take care of yourself, honey. Thanks for the call."

"You're welcome, Mom. Have a great day!"

Rebecca hung up as her throat tightened and tears pricked her eyes. Emptiness closed in on the familiar sense of joy and pride in her children. *Now what?* Her heart cried out to God. *What's next? Jim and I were always so excited about this time in our lives. Now he's gone too. What am I going to do?* Suddenly forty seemed so old, too old to start over and yet, too young to give up. Burying her face in the pillow, she let the tears flow.

I will never leave you nor forsake you.

Rebecca heard the words with rare clarity, as though Jesus were standing beside her. "That's great, Lord. But are You really here? You aren't standing by the bed where I can touch You. I can't see Your face or feel Your arms around me."

She waited. For what she didn't really know. Assurance? Confirmation? Peace?

Nothing.

She huffed a breath, swiped at her tears. "But I won't leave You and I won't give up if You don't leave me. No matter how hard it gets. That's a promise."

A soothing calmness washed over her as it had when Jim took her in his arms. Only this was different, deeper, and Rebecca knew the Lord was holding her. Again, the tears came, but this time they were of relief. "Thank You, O' God. Thank You."

She tucked Jim's pillow next to her heart, burrowed deeper into the mattress, and drifted off to dream once more in the early morning hours...

Warm, fragrant air skimmed her cheeks as the car made its way up the winding road. Lilacs bloomed. Clusters of purple in shrubs so green it made her eyes hurt—but in a good way. She took a deep breath and felt the smell of the air clear down to her soul. The scents dark, rich, and so full of flavor that she could almost taste them. Grapes and flowers and—

"She left everything to you."

Rebecca jerked awake at the voice from nowhere, sat up, and placed a palm against her thundering heart. She could still feel the balmy air on her cheeks and smell the rich fragrances in her mind. She ran a shaky hand through her hair and looked around. Safe, at home, in bed. Relief poured through her. "I must be losing my mind."

Throwing back the covers, she climbed from the beneath them, padded her way into the kitchen and turned on the coffee pot. While she waited for the aromatic liquid to brew, Rebecca put away her clean dishes then watered the ivy in the window. Her mind wandered back to the dream and the voice that woke her.

There was something achingly familiar about the place...the long winding road...the glint of silver in her rear-view mirror, like a reflection off glass or metal or something...the smell of lilacs and grapes...

Shaking off the memories, she flipped the devotional calendar to see what scripture was in store for her today.

I am the vine you are the branch, apart from me, you can do nothing. Once again, the scent of lilacs and grapes filled her mind, lingered in the air.

This is crazy. I can't even remember the last time—if ever—I've smelled lilacs or grapes, rich, ripe, and still on the vine. A chill washed over her skin. *I have to get out of here.* She poured her coffee into a travel mug, dressed, and went out to take a drive.

As if on automatic pilot, she backed out of the driveway, wound her way through the neighborhood then headed up Highway 18 toward North Bend and on to Snoqualmie Falls.

The radio announcer reported a heavy mist had rolled in off Puget Sound. If so, it would be burned away by the rapidly rising sun in a sky so clear she could see Mt. Baker on the horizon. Despite this, the promise of an early fall chilled the air. Rebecca lowered the window hoping the crisp breeze would help clear her mind.

Located between Snoqualmie and Fall City, Washington, Snoqualmie Falls ranged one hundred feet higher than Niagara but were not as vast. The spot had always been one of her favorite places to visit. There were trails leading to the bottom of the cascade, around it, and even featured lookouts strategically placed for those who had no desire to take a hike through the woods.

She parked her car, grabbed her jacket, and headed down a one-mile trek. The thick foliage of lush forestry surrounding the falls nearly eclipsed the bright morning sun. Rebecca knew her lack of exercise over the past year would require her to make several stops on her way back up the trail, but for now, she hurried toward the base.

Standing at the bottom, she looked up, awed by the splendid beauty of water tumbling over rock. Droplets bounced in the air like crystal prisms, reflecting sunlight in little bursts of color. Tiny rainbows danced on the wind.

Rebecca pulled the jacket tighter and sat on huge rock at the foot of a tree, hoping the majestic view would soothe her troubled mind. She took a deep breath and inhaled the crisp, clean mountain air, eager for it to wash away the tension.

Instead of the peace she craved, memories of the last time she and Jim came here crowded her mind. They had laughed and talked, teased, and flirted like teenagers, rather than people who'd been married twenty-plus years. Then he'd picked her up and feigned an attempt to throw her into the water.

Tears pricked her eyes and burned her throat. She stood and walked to the edge of the bank. Only a few feet separated her from the raging water below. *It would be so easy to slip into the water and disappear forever.* The words were clear, as though someone had whispered them in her ear. The thought, so dark, so menacing, so... tempting...

She took a deliberate step back.

Rebecca clutched her arms around her waist and considered once more that she must surely be losing her mind. A place known to remind one of God's glory, to refresh the soul and bring one back to life, a place she'd always enjoyed, held nothing but memories for her now. Memories that should've filled her with joy but wrenched her heart instead.

Not finding the solace she longed for, Rebecca turned from the bank and headed back up the trail. About halfway up, the muscles in her legs screamed for relief and she could no longer see through the tears blurring her vision. Sobs shook her shoulders and hindered her ability to put one foot in front of the other. She spotted a bench and crumbled onto it until spent, she could only pray for the strength to carry on.

Oh, God, what am I going to do? I feel so useless. Jim is gone. The kids are grown and pursuing their own dreams. I've never been anything but a housewife and mother. What do You have for me to do now?

"For I know the plans I have for you, a plan for your good, not for your destruction."

"That's great, Lord, but can you fill me in?" Rebecca tried to quiet her heart and mind, waiting for the Lord to show her what He had in store for her life. When He remained silent, His plan still a mystery, she knew the only thing left to do was to trust.

She made her way back up the trail and to her car then headed home. She walked onto the porch with a heartfelt sigh of relief. Never had she welcomed coming home to such degree. Not in the past year anyway. She reached for the mail in her box. Scent wafted from the packet of envelopes to tease her nostrils. Rebecca smiled. Her letter carrier had a habit of putting scented stickers on the mail.

What is that smell? She pressed the packet to her nose and took a deep, inhaling breath. *Lilacs.* Her hand trembled. She gripped the packet firmly to keep from dropping it, fumbled with her house key, and fought to open the door before her knees gave way.

Chapter Two

U. S. Postal Carrier Raymond Jacobey crossed the street as he watched Rebecca lift the mail to her nose. He smiled. He'd taken over this route less than a month after Mr. Sinclair passed away. From the moment Ray laid eyes on the little widow with jet-black hair and eyes so rich in color they reminded him of violets, she'd captured his heart.

At approximately five-feet-two inches, a raving beauty she was not. Her eyes were a bit too wide set, but fringed with thick, black lashes most women would die for. Her cheekbones were too high for the small, baby-like face and, as with most of the women he knew, she constantly battled with those infamous extra ten pounds. But something about her slightly rounded figure and soft features tugged at his heart. "Morning Ms. Sinclair."

"Hello Mr. Jacobey." Her voice trembled.

Ray noticed her wavering smile and the haunted look in her eyes. Concern skittered across his neck at the paleness of her complexion and the thin sheen of perspiration dotting her forehead. "Are you all right?"

Rebecca shrugged, swallowed hard. "A little stressed."

"Anything I can do for you?"

She wiped her brow with the back of her hand, shook her head and smiled. "Weird dreams and voices in the wind."

He grinned, hoping to relieve a little of her stress. "I thought that only happened to me."

A charming flush tinted her cheeks. "Well, it's never happened to me before. Can't say as I like it either. Would you like a cup of coffee or tea?"

"I'd love one." Raymond didn't hesitate. The house across from the Sinclair home was the last on his route before lunch. Many times, he'd accepted Rebecca's offer of coffee or tea, hoping to ease the sting of loneliness that clouded those pretty indigo eyes. He put down his mailbag, sat on the porch swing and waited while she brewed them each a cup.

He'd learned a lot about Rebecca Sinclair in the past year. Married at seventeen, she'd followed her husband across the country during his twenty years in the Air Force. Upon retirement, Jim Sinclair had taken a position at the aircraft plant in Seattle, working as a mechanic on the huge engines used to propel the big jets. Her oldest child, a son named Jeffrey, graduated high school three years ago and moved to New York to pursue an acting career. Her youngest, Debbie, graduated this past May and now attended college in France.

In one of their conversations, Rebecca confided that she'd been shy as a child. Marriage at such a young age and the constant moving during her husband's Air Force career hadn't made it easy for her to make or maintain many friendships. Now that her children were grown and there were no more ball games, band concerts, or PTA meetings, she had no idea what to do next.

Raymond's heart ached for her and had he the intestinal fortitude to ask—and if she said yes—he'd gladly marry her and give her plenty to do for the rest of her life. Need curled in the pit of his stomach at the thought, and once again he felt the familiar sense of frustration at his own shyness and insecurity.

~*~

In the kitchen, Rebecca brewed a fresh pot of coffee. She knew their visits usually consumed most of his lunch hour, so she made sandwiches and thought about what she'd learned regarding Raymond Jacobey in the last year.

A wanderer at heart, his biggest desire was to see the world. Flat feet kept him out of the military so, fresh out of high school Raymond obtained his first job with the U.S. Post Office in his hometown.

Whenever wanderlust took hold, he'd pick several places on the map, send in resumes, and then wait for a job offer. Once he received one, he'd put in for a transfer and move on to continue his career in a whole new state, city, or town, which enabled him to see some of the country in which he resided. He seldom stayed in one place more than a year or so and occasionally took a college course or two, but that was as deep as his roots went in any given place.

In the past eighteen years, he'd lived in fifteen different locations.

Rebecca put away the sandwich ingredients and smiled as Ray's image swam before her eyes.

He wasn't a big man, five-feet-eight-inches or so and though not male model material, he was incredibly cute and sweet. His sandy-blond hair constantly needed a trim, but he always sported a smile and his gold-flecked green eyes danced with humor and joy. His shoulders were broad, his arms muscular, not bulging but well-proportioned for his height. His legs were slender and well-toned from the walking he did, and he sported a healthy tan all year around.

Little did he know it, but he'd saved her life more than once in the past year. He'd always made a point of talking with her and never left the mail without making sure she was up and about and doing OK. He'd stayed to share a cup of coffee with her on more than one occasion.

She had a hunch his feelings for her went deeper than plain friendship, but having been married over half of her life, Rebecca had no idea what to do or how she felt in return. One thing was certain, with his friendly smile and laughing green eyes, she looked forward to seeing him every day, especially now that Debbie was off to school.

She poured the coffee in a decorative carafe to keep it hot and placed it on a large serving tray alongside cups, sugar and cream, the sandwiches, and two glasses of milk.

As she walked back out on the porch, his smile welcomed her. Ray rose from the swing, took the tray and set it on the small patio table, and then waited for her to curl up in the rocking chair as she usually did before resuming his seat.

He reached for a sandwich and glass of milk. "You didn't have to go to all this trouble."

"It's no trouble, makes me feel useful and needed again." Her voice cracked with emotion.

The gentle light in his eyes matched his tender grin. "Well, in that case, I'll expect lunch every day."

Rebecca couldn't help but smile in return. "Oh, really?"

"It's my job to serve, Ma'am," he said in his most professional voice. "And if serving me lunch makes you feel needed and useful, then I'm more than happy to oblige," he assured with a chuckle.

"I'll keep that in mind."

"Now, you want to tell me about those weird dreams and voices in the wind?"

Rebecca frowned as the dream came back with vivid clarity. "Ever dream about someplace and when you wake up, swear you've been there before?"

"Sometimes. Is that what happened?"

She nodded.

"What about those voices you mentioned, part of the dream?"

"Sort of, but not really. There was a voice in the dream. It's what woke me. But the voice in the wind was different. Dark, menacing, it tempted me to dive into Snoqualmie Falls." She shivered at the memory. "I feel like I'm losing my mind."

For a moment, Rebecca thought Ray was going to pull her into his arms, and her heart dropped an uncharacteristic beat at the thought. Instead, he leaned over and placed his hand over her trembling one.

"You're not losing your mind."

"Then what's wrong with me?" She held back a sob, willing the quiver in her voice to steady.

His eyes reflected kindness and understanding as he gazed at her, the warmth of his hand on hers more comforting than she'd have imagined.

"As for the place in the dream, you've probably visited it sometime or another in your life. Or maybe you've seen it on TV or read about it in a book. Hence, the reason it seems so familiar. And the voice, well that's the voice of grief trying to convince you to give up instead of moving on with your life. I, for one, am glad you didn't listen to it."

His voice gentled, became a balm. "It's been a year, Rebecca, don't you think it's time for you to start letting go and move forward?"

"And do what? All I've ever been, is a housewife and mother. I have no skills other than those needed to maintain a home and family and no education outside of the G.E.D. I received after I was married. What good am I anymore?"

"I'm sure God has plans for you, Becca, and I'm sure He'll reveal them in His own perfect time. Just be patient and promise me you won't give up." His gaze held hers in a tender plea.

"I promise." She sighed. "Guess it's just a turning forty thing."

He smiled again and gave her hand a gentle squeeze. "Who's turning forty, surely not you?"

She gave him a look and he chuckled.

"When?"

"Today."

"Why didn't you tell me? I'd have bought you lunch instead of allowing you to wait on me."

"Oh, and how do you suppose I should have done that?" She arched an eyebrow. "Just come out and say, 'oh, by-the-way, tomorrow's my birthday?'"

Ray grinned. "Forty is just a number. Besides, haven't you heard that life begins at forty?"

"That's what I used to think. Now, I'm not so sure. At this point, forty feels like a hundred, like I'm too young to quit and too old to start over."

"Nonsense, women are doing all sorts of new things at forty nowadays, even fifty. Have you thought about going back to school?"

She shook her head, grateful for the change of subject. Their visit continued on a much lighter note than it began, and before long, consumed his entire lunch hour, and then some. With obvious reluctance, he left to continue his route. Rebecca waved goodbye then returned to the kitchen to clean up the few dishes from the morning. Her heart did a slow swirl to her stomach as she remembered the softness in his eyes and voice when he'd called her 'Becca.'

No one had ever called her Becca.

The thought occurred to her once more that his feelings for her went far deeper than friendship.

Closing her eyes, she could feel his hand on hers again. Her heart reached her stomach and did a little flip. Heat flooded her entire being. She took a deep breath, opened her eyes, and tried to quell the butterflies dancing along every nerve in her body.

Not only was she *not* losing her mind, but she was also very much alive.

Rebecca shook off the foolishness of her thoughts, went into the living room, sat in her favorite chair—a huge rocking recliner with cushions so thick she felt as though she were sinking into a cloud—and opened her Bible to continue reading where she'd left off the day before. The Gospel of John, chapter fifteen leapt out at her...*I am the vine, and my Father is the vine grower...I am the vine you are the branches. Whoever remains in me and I in him will bear much fruit because without me you can do nothing...*

She paused in her reading. "God, what is it about vines and branches? I know You're trying to show me something, but what?"

Once again, she was in her dream...the long winding road...the glint of silver in her rear-view mirror...the scent of lilacs and grapes.

Raymond's words echoed in her mind, *"I'm sure God has plans for you, Becca, and I'm sure He'll reveal them in His own perfect time. Just be patient."*

The hair on the back of her neck stood up. Goose bumps rose on her flesh. Rebecca got out of her chair and down on her knees.

~*~

Raymond pulled out of the parking lot and headed to the YMCA. Though exhausted, he looked forward to his daily swim. He changed from his uniform into swim trunks and sandals, rinsed in the shower then strode to edge of the pool, kicked off his shoes, and dove in. Warm water caressed his flesh. The muscles in his shoulders and back bunched and flexed to the rhythmic motion as he stroked and kicked his way from one end of the structure to the other, easing the tension from his body and mind.

The long lunch and his preoccupation with Rebecca had caused him to run late the remainder of his route. Leaving her today had been one of the most difficult tasks of his life. Several times during the afternoon, he'd walked up to a house only to realize that he had the wrong packet of mail in his hand.

Instead of enjoying the benefits of additional walking, the return trips to the vehicle to exchange one resident's mail for the correct bundle only served to increase his frustration. By the time he returned to the main hub, completed his paperwork, and traded the mail truck for his personal SUV, every muscle in his body was in knots. The pool helped.

Being with Rebecca would've helped more.

After an hour of swimming laps in the heated, indoor pool, he headed home in a much calmer frame of mind. Raymond gathered the ingredients and cookware he needed and then set about preparing his dinner. He peeled potatoes and cut them into neat, round slices and then layered them along with meat, seasoning and onions into a casserole dish. As flavors permeated the kitchen, he thought about his life. Hailing from Flagstaff, Arizona, he'd always thought of himself as a small fish in a big pond. With a population of more than fifty thousand, Flagstaff was a far cry from the small-town life he longed for. The magnetism of the nearby Grand Canyon made it a year-round attraction for visitors and increased the number of people crowding the already densely populated area.

He had nothing against the beautiful city at the base of the San Francisco Peaks, but Ray craved the intimacy and community—the quiet, unhurried, idyllic lifestyle—offered in smaller towns. That was why every time he relocated, he chose small towns or suburbs of the larger cities. Dayton, Texas, a stone's throw from Houston. Welsh, Louisiana, a mere twenty miles from Lake Charles. Kent, Washington, only forty- five minutes from Seattle.

Ray finished the dinner preparations, slid the dish into the oven, set the timer, and allowed his mind to wander along the path of his childhood. The only offspring of high-powered executives, he always felt alone while growing up. Oh, he had everything a boy could want, computers, video games, expensive clothes, but the one thing he wanted most—the love and support of family—was the one thing he lacked.

In all of his thirty-eight years, Raymond hadn't met two people less cut out for parenting than his mother and father. They weren't cruel people, just busy living life with the passion that was a by-product of their environment. They played as fervently as they worked, fought as strongly as they loved, loved as passionately as they hated. Neither of them understood the shy, quiet boy who was their son. Had they been as zealous about parenting as they were about everything else, maybe they would have understood, or at least appreciated him, and maybe he wouldn't have been so lonely.

His fists clenched in automatic defense against the memories—the fights, the insults, the screaming followed by passionate embraces. The helpless feeling of being trapped in a world where he didn't belong.

How could he—who was the exact opposite of everything they were—have come from such extreme, fanatical, obsessive human beings? Where they were zealous, he was calm. They were extreme, he was conservative. They were boisterous and he was shy.

A loner they called him, a drifter with a deep-rooted wanderlust that was the antithesis of their excessive need to be in control of their destiny and to dominate everything and everyone within their power.

But Raymond knew differently. Wanderlust was not what drove him from place to place, but the age-old search for the ever-elusive soul mate—someone who would love and respect and nurture him, and the children he hoped to have, for who they were without trying to mold them into little replicas of herself.

The timer on the oven chimed. Ray removed the casserole and set it on the counter to cool while he set the table. His mind went back to lunch. His heart ached remembering the pain and fear in Rebecca's eyes. The sorrow and loneliness in her gaze cried out to the deepest part of him, and Raymond knew he'd finally found his soul mate.

Problem was, he had absolutely no idea what to do with the knowledge.

How soon was too soon for the lovely widow to get on with her life? How long should he wait before pursuing the woman of his dreams?

Had he a deeper relationship with his father, Ray would call him and ask for advice. Instead, he bowed his head to speak to *the* Father. "Lord, give me wisdom and patience, but above all, Lord, give me boldness when the time is right."

A sense of calm purpose settled over him, and Ray knew God would direct his steps and make straight his paths.

Chapter Three

Rebecca stretched groggily and opened her eyes to meet the morning. After several hours in prayer yesterday, the afternoon and evening passed without incident. Along with her lunch with Ray, the call from her son wishing her a happy birthday, followed by a call and a letter from her daughter doing the same were the highlights of her day.

Rebecca spent hours penning her responding letter, pouring her heart out to Debbie in assurance that she was fine, doing well and looking forward to the holidays.

Lies.

Every one of the carefully orchestrated sentences was a lie. She was not looking forward to endless nights alone during a typical, long Washington winter. Except for the fact that her children would be home at Christmas, she dreaded the upcoming holidays.

She threw back the covers, climbed from the bed, kicked the thermostat up a notch, and went into the kitchen. Hoping a bit of sunshine would chase away her blues, she glanced out the window only to be disappointed.

Though nature had defied the weatherman yesterday and blessed them with an unseasonably beautiful day, today the heavens succumbed to the very definition of fall. Gray mist hung in the overcast sky. Thick clouds billowed over the mountains bringing the promise of rain or snow or both.

Rebecca picked up her letter to Debbie and seriously considered tearing it up and starting over. What would her daughter say if she knew how her mother really felt about being alone in this big house with nothing but memories for company?

She collapsed into a chair and clenched her fists. Debbie would feel obligated to come home and keep her mother company. Rebecca would not have that on her conscience. Especially since her daughter had worked so hard to be accepted into the most prestigious university in Paris. She pressed the heels of her hands into her eyes and fought back tears. *Lord, I refuse to be in this mood again today.*

She flipped the daily devotional calendar and read the Scripture of the day: *Rejoice, and again I say rejoice knowing that your trials and suffering brings about patience.*

Help me, Lord. Help me to rejoice in You, Rebecca pleaded from the bottom of her heart. Scriptures of hope and healing came to mind: *He has given us the garment of praise for the spirit of heaviness. A joyful heart is the health of the body, but a depressed spirit dries up the bones.*

Words rose from somewhere in the depths of her troubled soul, *the joy of the Lord is my strength...* Rebecca's smile trembled as the chorus reverberated in her heart. Rising from her chair, she turned on the radio and opened the curtains. This is the day that the Lord has made and gray sky or blue I will rejoice and be glad.

Within moments, the song in her spirit resounded from the radio speakers and filled the melancholy atmosphere with optimism. Joy rose within her. Rebecca found herself smiling and laughing and dancing around the kitchen. She glided through the house, opened the curtains, and turned on all the radios, tuning them to the same station until the house resounded with songs of faith.

Before long, she'd changed clothes, put her hair in a ponytail and cleaned the house. That done, she rolled up her sleeves and immersed herself in deep cleaning the appliances as she sang along with the music. A knock on the front door startled her. Elbow deep in defrosting the freezer, she nearly bumped her head. With a renewed spirit and sense of purpose, she opened the door to Ray's smiling face. "Hi."

"Hi." He had the strangest look on his face. Rebecca cocked her head. "Are you OK?"

He grinned. "Yeah, you just caught me daydreaming."

"Daydreaming about what?"

His eyebrow arched in a teasing gesture. "Getting kinda personal, aren't you?"

His green eyes danced with wicked humor. Rebecca's cheeks grew hot.

Ray chuckled. "No lunch today?"

"No. I'm cleaning out the freezer. But it will only take a minute to throw something together."

Ray laughed. "Don't bother. I'll grab a burger later."

"I told you yesterday it's no bother. At least let me fix you a cup of coffee."

He nodded in agreement and settled on the porch swing to wait. Rebecca studied him for a brief moment before closing the door. His grin reminded her of a love-struck teen on a first date. That look couldn't be for her, could it? A tiny thrill raced through her at the thought, quickly followed by a tug of guilt. She made her way to the kitchen to pour a couple cups of coffee and all the frustrations of yesterday vanished, replaced by the unexpected image of spending winter nights curled up by the fire with Ray. Where had that come from? She was still having a difficult time getting used to being without Jim, and her heart still ached with love for her husband. How could the image of another man invade her mind?

"It's been a year, Becca...." Ray's words from yesterday swept the cobwebs of guilt from her heart. Life goes on, she thought. She forced the image and her thoughts from her mind and focused on pouring coffee and putting out a few pastries. When she emerged from the house carrying a tray, she smiled at Ray.

He stood and took the tray, set it on the table and waited for her to curl up in the rocking chair before settling on the swing once more. He reached for a pastry and a cup of coffee. "Ummm, dessert first. I like that idea."

Rebecca giggled. "The mother in me cringes at the thought of ruining your appetite with sweets, but since I lost track of time and forgot you insisted I fix lunch every day, it's the best I could do."

The look of admiration he gave her stole her breath.

"You look good today."

Rebecca glanced down at her baggy sweat pants and oversized, faded denim shirt. "You have a strange idea of what 'looking good' means. I can promise you I won't be leaving the house dressed like this."

Ray threw his napkin at her. "I'm not talking about the clothes. I'm talking about the person in them."

Feeling like a giddy schoolgirl, she laughed again.

"Since you're so cheerful this morning, I take it you had a better night last night than the one before?" He sipped his coffee.

"Not really. I got up in a terrible mood but refused to stay in it. The Bible says that God inhabits the praise of His people and in all things we should give Him praise. So basically, I praised myself into a better frame of mind."

"Good for you, worked too. You're certainly much prettier with a smile on your lips and a light in your eyes."

A blush heated her cheeks. "Thank you." She captured his gaze with a pointed look and fought back a wave of insecurity. "Are you flirting with me, Raymond?"

He pierced her with a steady gaze. "I don't know, Becca. What do you think?"

There it was again, *Becca*. The name flowed over her like a caress, but the flash of insecurity in his eyes surprised her. He was a strong and vital man. She wouldn't have expected her insecurity to be mirrored in him, but it tugged at her heart and conjured a protective instinct. She smiled and forced her voice to be light. "I think you're a very sweet man who has a way of making a woman feel special even when she is dressed like a bum."

Not sure what or if she should say anything else, she rose from her seat and reached for the tray.

"Let me," he insisted. His hand grazed hers in an intimate scrape of flesh against flesh.

Awareness sizzled between them, shocked her in its intensity.

He took the tray from her trembling grasp then gave her an innocent grin and nodded toward the door. "After you, Ma'am."

Rebecca led the way to the kitchen as gracefully as possible on legs that wobbled. She turned towards him as he set the tray on the counter.

"By the way, who do you know from New York?"

A quick spirt of laughter preceded her words. "You

mean other than my son?"

He shook his head, pulled an envelope out of his shirt pocket, and held it toward her. "Not *City*, Hammondsport."

She frowned, shook her head, and reached for the envelope. "What?"

"See, the return address says Hammondsport, New York." He handed her the envelope.

Rebecca stared at the return address, searching her mind. Jeffrey hadn't said anything about going to Hammondsport. Not that she could remember anyway. Still, the name had a familiar ring to it. A fleeting thought—more like a memory that wouldn't fully form—crossed her mind, lingered then gelled. She felt the blood drain from her face. Her hand trembled. "That's it," she whispered. "Ray, that's it." She focused on his face, all warmth from hers gone.

"What?" he asked, a worried frown creasing his brow.

"The dream. The house."

Ray shook his head. "Are you saying you've been there or know someone who has?"

Rebecca ran a shaky hand over her head. "I don't know," she murmured, but the rapid beat of her heart told her she should. She closed her eyes and recalled the dream...*the long winding road, the glint of silver in her rear-view mirror...the scent of grapes and lilacs.*

A picture began to take shape in her mind...an old woman standing in the doorway of a big house...a young woman of heartbreaking beauty, thin, fragile, dark hair flying in the wind, sobs shaking her slender frame... *"Look at her and tell me she's not his!"*

She pointed to the little girl clinging to her skirt. Tugging the child from behind her, the young woman jerked around to face the old one once more.

"She looks just like him!" she insisted, gripping the little girl's hand.

Her hand.

Chapter Four

Rebecca dropped the envelope. "It can't be..." Her voice trailed off in a whisper.

Fear, unlike anything Ray had ever known curled in the pit of his stomach. "Can't be what?"

Rebecca covered her face with trembling hands. "What's happening? Why now? Why her?"

Ray touched her arm. "You're making absolutely no sense, Rebecca, and you're scaring the daylights out of me."

"Wait here," she said, and bolted from the room.

Stunned by her reaction, Ray stood on leaden legs and forced himself to pick up the envelope. Then he collapsed onto the nearest chair. He stood when she entered the room, noting how her hand shook when she put down the cigar box she carried and how the paleness still lingered on her face. Afraid she might faint he jerked a chair out from the table and urged her into it.

She clutched her hands in her lap and put her head next to the box.

Bypassing the coffee, he walked over to the refrigerator and sighed with relief when his eyes fell on a bottle of wine. Fumbling through the drawers for a corkscrew, he uncorked it, poured her a glass, and set it in front of her.

"Drink," he said. "It will steady your nerves."

Rebecca obeyed without even a whimper of protest. Her hands steadied and color returned to her cheeks.

"Now, you want to tell me what's going on?"

"Jesus, help me." The prayer from Rebecca's lips was

almost inaudible as she reached for the box, hesitated then pushed the container toward Ray.

He removed the rubber band holding the cardboard together, the slender strip so old it crumbled in his hand. He dumped the remains on the table. Lifting the fragile lid of the box, he noted the slim contents within...Rebecca's birth certificate, and her mother's, her father's dog tags, a diary, a letter. The return address on the yellow packet matched the address on the envelope that started this whole episode. "Your father's family?"

"Either that or the executor of the estate."

"Do you know these people? Have you ever met them?"

Rebecca shook her head. "I'm not sure. I have this impression, but it seems so surreal, more like a dream than a memory."

"Tell me about it." He hoped he wasn't pushing too hard, but he knew sometimes talking had a way of helping a person work things out in his or her mind. Besides, he wanted to know everything about her.

"My mother died when I was four, so I had to be very young, two or three maybe. I remember clinging to her skirt while she cried. There was an old woman standing in the doorway of a big house. She was..." Rebecca hesitated, as if letting the memory fully form.

"There was something mean-spirited about her. She frightened me." She shuddered and took a deep breath.

"Anyway, I remember my mother saying something about the way I looked and urging the old woman, whom I'm assuming is or was my grandmother, to look at me and deny that I looked like him. *Him*, I'm guessing, is my father."

Rebecca drained the remaining wine from her glass, put

it down and buried her face in her hands. "It's funny how a child assimilates things and then forgets them. Strange it should all come back to me. Like something out of an old movie."

Again, she shuddered, closed her eyes, and took a deep breath. "I remember the smell of grapes, so rich, so ripe and sweet. And lilacs." She smiled a little. "I remember sneaking some on the way back to the car and thinking that I'd paid the old lady back for making my mama cry."

Ray chuckled and pushed the letter toward her. "Are you going to open this?"

Rebecca's hand shook as she reached for the envelope. On a surge, she shoved it away. "Why should I? She never cared about me, so what difference does it make what she has to say now? Why should I care after all these years?"

He'd never felt truly loved or wanted by his parents, so Ray understood all too well why Rebecca would think this. He remained silent for a few minutes. "So, what will you do?"

In a quick decisive move, Rebecca picked up the envelope and tossed it into the box. "Put it in here with all the other bad memories." She closed the lid and pushed it away.

Ray's heart trembled with the need to pull her in his arms, to comfort her and take away the pain he saw reflected in her eyes. But he feared, as much as desired, the feel of her soft body against his. Feared that if he brought her near, he would forever be lost, and now was not the time to reveal his feelings, not while she was fragile, and his lunch hour was almost over.

Still, he couldn't resist one more touch and enveloped her hand in his. "I really hate to leave you right now, but I have to get back to my route. Will you be OK?"

When she nodded, he lifted her hand and pressed his lips to the back, squeezed in a gesture of comfort and support then rose from his seat. "Good. Thank you for the coffee and the pastry."

"You're welcome." Rebecca's voice quivered.

He walked out of the house to continue his route.

"Wait!" she called, rushing after him.

In his mind's eye, she was running toward him with open arms. Paralyzed with fear and need, Raymond stayed seated in his truck, doubting his legs would hold him should he get out of the vehicle.

Rebecca held out an envelope. "I almost forgot to give this to you," she gasped, obviously breathless from the sprint.

Taking it, Ray looked dumbly at the envelope in his hand. "Oh," he muttered, feeling foolish and embarrassed at his own thoughts.

She skimmed her lips across his cheek. "Thank you, Ray. You've been a wonderful friend to me these past months."

Ray fought the urge to bolt from the truck, drag her into his arms and confess his love. Taking a deep breath, he resisted the impulse to raise the letter to his nose to see if her scent lingered on the paper. Forcing the heart from his throat he placed it firmly on his sleeve. Fear of rejection made his bones ache. Still, he took the chance. "I'd like to be more than your friend, Becca."

"I thought you might. I'm not sure how I feel about that yet. I've been married over half my life, widowed barely a year. I have no idea how to go about being single." Her voice was soft, her smile tender.

"But you're not opposed to the idea?"

She touched his cheek with her fingertips. "No. I'm not opposed to the idea." She stepped back from the curb. "Go to work, and we'll talk some more tomorrow," she promised and then turned back toward the house.

"Becca?"

She stopped and faced him once more.

"I'm not good at anything but being single. I promise to take it slow. I would never want to hurt you or rush you or scare you away."

She smiled. "Thank you. I'll see you tomorrow."

Raymond's heart soared. He nodded and eased his truck from the curb. He finished his route, worked out, and, as usual, had supper alone. But like a kid on Christmas Eve, he couldn't wait for morning to dawn.

Chapter Five

Unable to sleep, Rebecca lay awake, and stared into space. A small night-light in the bathroom illuminated the darkness. She'd dozed fitfully since retiring late the evening before. Her body ached from the cleaning spree she'd embarked on.

After she'd finished defrosting the freezer, she'd tackled the kitchen cabinets and then the utility room, after which she stripped and waxed the floor of both. She'd stretched and climbed and scrubbed more in those few hours than she had in over a year.

Christian music interspersed with teaching programs had kept her heart focused while her hands worked. At odd little moments, the memory of lunch with Raymond would come to mind, making her smile. The day had been full, taxing, but she'd enjoyed it.

Her evening hadn't been as productive though. She'd tried to continue her Bible reading but couldn't seem to get past the Gospel of John. Her prayer time had been interrupted with thoughts of the letter she'd received followed by memories of her conversation with Raymond.

Even now, he crowded her mind...the softness in his eyes, and the thrill of his touch. What would it be like to be married to him?

Climbing from beneath the covers, she walked to her dresser, lit the candle there, and then returned to her bed. Rebecca propped the pillows behind her, folded her hands and bowed her head. *God, is this what You want from me, to be a wife again?*

Part of her thrilled at the idea of having a husband once more, someone to cook for, someone to look after, possibly another baby or two. Being a wife and mother was all she knew how to do. Rebecca prided herself on the fact that she'd been good at it, but part of her cringed at the thought.

Though Jim had been a wonderful husband, they'd had their share of problems. Twenty years in the Air Force instilled in him a strong sense of order. He, in turn, expected the same of her. Things had to be in their place. The house had to be clean. Clutter was unacceptable.

Many times, Rebecca had thought she would suffocate from his constant need for order. But she loved him and tried her best to make him happy. If there were times when she was vaguely dissatisfied, wondering if there was more to life than being a wife and mother, she'd squashed those feelings with ruthless determination. She tried always to be grateful for the gifts God had given her.

Despite his need for organization, he hadn't been abusive in any way. He'd never verbally or physically struck her or the children. Jim had been a good man and a good provider who loved, honored, and cherished her. He'd been faithful, gentle, and respectful.

Could anyone compare to that? Would marriage to another be the same as before? Better? Worse? Once again, Raymond's face rose in her mind followed by a nagging sensation that—though he may be a part of it—God had something different in store for the rest of her life. *But what?*

Restless, she got out of bed, blew out the candle and went into the kitchen. Putting the kettle on to boil, she dug through her box of herbal teas for a bag of chamomile, hoping its calming qualities would help her relax and get to sleep.

She ran a tub of warm water adding bath crystals that were supposed to induce relaxation. Lighting an aromatherapy candle she then returned to the kitchen, prepared the cup of tea, and carried it back into the bathroom. While the bag steeped its soothing flavor into the mug, Rebecca twisted her hair on top of her head and secured it with a clip. Remembering how Jim had insisted they get back to nature and sank into the water with a smile. Herbal teas, herbal baths, and aromatherapy candles were just some of the ways they did so. Others included using fresh herbs in place of processed seasonings, drinking filtered water instead of tap and implementing massage therapy to aide each other in relaxation.

"God put those plants on earth for our benefit," he'd said, and as usual, she had listened. Healthy though they were, herbal teas were an acquired taste, but it hadn't taken long for them to reap the benefits.

Rebecca closed her eyes and slid further into the tub as she sipped. Her body began to unwind. Her mind wandered back over the years to the many nights Jim had fixed her a cup of tea and a bubble bath. How he'd carried her from the tub to the bed and rubbed scented oil into her skin. The warmth of his hands, the scents of the candles he'd lit and the intimacy that always followed brought blissful memories. Being a wife and mother, Rebecca never thought of herself as a sensual creature. Jim tried hard to show her otherwise.

Shocked at the path her thoughts had taken, Rebecca's eyes jerked open. She sat upright. Her hand trembled when she put down the teacup. Though she'd wished many times that her husband had taken her with him on that fateful day when he died, she was now very much aware she was far from deceased.

God, thank You so much for reminding me I'm still alive. But Lord, I don't think these are the kind of feelings I should be having considering the fact that I am a widow and currently alone.

Embarrassed at her thoughts, Rebecca rose from the tub, reached for a towel, and draped it securely around her. "Now I need a cold shower," she grumbled, and then laughed out loud.

She'd often wondered whether the benefits of a cold shower were fact or fiction, but even with her body on fire, she dared not try it. The idea of being cold and wet on purpose was distasteful.

She reached for pajamas. Sleep would be impossible now, so she bypassed the pajamas, walked into the bedroom, dug out a pair of sweats and a T- shirt. Ingrained habit had her scrubbing the oily film from the tub before she left the room. Even on those nights when Jim had swept her up in his arms and carried her from the bathroom, once the romance was over and the passion spent, she would climb out of bed or get up early to make sure the tub was clean for his shower the next day.

Edgy and restless, Rebecca roamed through the house. The clock chimed. Three o'clock in the morning—too early to get up, too late to go back to bed. She wandered into the living room, sat in her recliner, and picked up her Bible. Once again it opened to the Gospel of John, chapter 15...*I am the vine, and my Father is the vine grower...I am the vine you are the branches. Whoever remains in me and I in him will bear much fruit because without me you can do nothing...*

"Jesus, what are You trying to tell me?" Too jittery to calm her mind or spirit enough to hear from God, she put down the Bible with a sigh and got up to roam the house once more. Within moments, she found herself in the room her husband had used as a gym.

Though she had always been careful with her diet and had regularly joined Jim on walks and hikes, she'd never been keen on exercising. Jim was the workout fanatic. She ran her hand over the equipment as she walked around the room. A bow machine for strength training, an exercise bike, treadmill, and rowing machine for cardiovascular.

Tears pricked her eyes. How on earth had a heart attack killed her husband when he'd taken such excellent care of himself?

She sat on the stationary bike, pedaled a few strokes. Boring. Though she'd enjoyed biking with her kids, Rebecca couldn't imagine how anyone withstood the monotony of pedaling for hours and going nowhere. Getting up, she walked over to the bow machine then cringed at the thought of adding insult to injury to her already aching muscles. The treadmill beckoned.

Before she could change her mind, Rebecca hurried into the bedroom, put on socks and tennis shoes, and returned to the workout room.

Barely understanding the basics of operating the electric walking machine, she put the key into the slot and slowly adjusted the speed until she moved at a brisk pace. *Now this I could get used to.* She laughed, realizing instead of pedaling, she was walking without going anywhere.

The benefits of jogging came to mind—improved cardiovascular health, lower cholesterol, increased metabolism, and the rumored 'runner's high.' The most running she'd ever done was chasing after kids. Rebecca coaxed the speed up a notch.

As her heart rate increased, the tension in her body lessened and her spirit soared. *Lord, this is great! All these years, and I never knew how wonderful this could be. Add a little music and visual imagery and even the stationary bike might be a pleasant thing.* She increased the speed yet again. Sweat poured off her brow and her lungs screamed for air.

Rebecca gradually decreased the speed to a slow, steady pace once more. Grasping the handrails, closed her eyes, she took deep breaths until her heart rate and breathing returned to normal.

The clock chimed four. She'd been on the treadmill for a little more than half an hour. Not wanting to overdo it, she decreased the speed until the machine slowed enough for her to stop the device.

Coated with sweat, Rebecca's heart pumped, and muscles quivered, but she couldn't recall a time in the past year when she felt more alive.

Jim had told her it was important to cool off gradually and stretch those warm muscles, so she took the time to do so. Disliking the sticky feel of cotton clinging to her flesh, she decided to take a shower. Standing under the spray of hot, pulsating water Rebecca marveled at how good she felt—energized and relaxed all at once. She emerged from the bathroom warm, cozy and refreshed. Donning clean clothes, she moseyed into the kitchen and turned on the coffee pot and watered her plants while the pot brewed. Pouring a cup, she went into the living room, curled up in her chair and turned on the television.

She awoke sometime later to the sound of someone pounding on her front door.

Chapter Six

Raymond knocked again and counted to ten.

It wasn't like Rebecca not to answer the door. Did she regret their conversation from yesterday? Was she avoiding him today? Maybe she wasn't home.

He walked to the garage and peered in the window. Her car was parked inside. She was home. He strode back onto the porch, put her mail in the box and turned away. He'd taken two steps when the door opened behind him.

"Ray?"

He turned. She stood in the doorway, flushed, and tousled.

"You're still sleeping." He grimaced at how ridiculous it sounded to state the obvious and tried again. "Are you OK?"

She scraped the hair out of her eyes. "I didn't sleep well last night, must have dozed off while watching TV."

"Oh. I was kind of worried." He ground his teeth in frustration. He'd opened his heart to her yesterday, and here he was getting all panicked and tongue-tied because she hadn't come to the door when he first knocked.

"Sorry, I'm still groggy. Can we talk tomorrow?"

"Tomorrow is my day off. If you give me your number, we can talk. But, I'd hoped we could have dinner tonight."

Rebecca grimaced.

Ray's hopes fizzled. "Never mind, I don't want you to feel pressured."

"No, wait." She gave him a genuine smile. "I'm sorry. I'm stiff and sore from cleaning the house yesterday and getting on the treadmill this morning. So now, I'm a bit disoriented from falling asleep in my chair. Dinner would be nice."

He took a step closer. "Where would you like to go?"

Her smile widened. "Someplace casual, I'm not sure I could struggle into a dress or pantyhose or walk in heels tonight."

Ray hesitated and reached for her hand. "We could make it another night, Becca," he offered, not wanting to appear insensitive to her discomfort.

"You're so sweet. I'm sure I'll be fine."

"OK. Can I pick you up at seven or do you want to meet me somewhere?"

"Would you prefer it if I meet you?"

He chuckled, shook his head. "I'm a traditional kind of guy. I'd prefer to pick you up, but whatever makes you most comfortable is fine with me."

"In that case, seven is fine. I'll see you later."

Raymond lifted her hand to his mouth and brushed his lips across her knuckles. "Until later, then. A tepid bath in Epson salts and a couple of pain reliever tablets might help those sore muscles."

Rebecca smiled. "Thank you. Have a good afternoon."

Ray worked the rest of his shift, swam laps, and then hurried home to shower and change. All afternoon he'd thought about where he would take her to dinner.

Opening the refrigerator for a cold drink, he spotted the steaks he'd picked up at the grocery store yesterday and smiled as an idea came to mind. Seasoning the steaks and leaving them to marinate, he tossed a salad, prepared potatoes to bake and set the table for two. He'd bought a bottle of wine like the one she had in her refrigerator, and although he had no clue how often—or even if—she drank with dinner, he put it in a bucket of ice to chill just in case.

Excitement curled in his soul as he drove to Rebecca's house.

~*~

Rebecca dressed with care, a pair of navy slacks, pale blue blouse, and casual pumps. She washed and styled her hair, added a touch of mascara to her dark lashes, a tinge of blush on her cheeks and a hint of color to her lips. The ache in her muscles had lessened to mild discomfort and she looked forward to the evening ahead. The phone rang just as she finished her toiletry. She glanced at the caller ID then picked up the receiver.

"Hi, Jeff."

"Hi, Mom!" Her son's voice boomed over the connection. "What'cha doin'?"

"I'm getting ready to go out to dinner."

"Where ya goin'?"

Rebecca hesitated a moment. "Actually, I'm not sure. A friend invited me to dinner but didn't say where we'd be going."

"Anyone I know?"

"I don't think so," she answered, unsure whether he'd ever met Ray.

"Sounds clandestine."

Rebecca laughed at the tease in his voice. "Clandestine? Me? You're kidding, right? Or maybe your imagination is in overdrive from too much playacting."

Jeff chuckled. "Well, are you going to dinner with a male

or female friend?"

"Male."

"So, it is a date. What's his name?"

Rebecca heard the change in her son's tone. "His name's Ray and he's a very nice man whom I've known for several months." She hoped to soothe her son's mind and ease his worrying, although she wasn't sure why. With middle-age hitting her head-on, she was pretty sure she could go out to dinner without her son's permission. Before she could offer any further explanation, a knock sounded on the door. "He's here. I've got to go, sweetheart. Have a good night."

"You too, Mom and be careful."

Rebecca hung up a bit concerned at the hesitancy in her son's voice, but she didn't have time to ponder long before the second knock came. She hurried to open the door.

"Evening, Ms. Sinclair. You look mighty nice for a casual dinner."

Rebecca eyed Ray's crisply starched shirt and slacks. Gold pinstripes in the pale green cotton shirt brought out flecks of the same shade in his eyes. The shine on his shoes reminded her of the meticulous way Jim had always buffed and polished his to an immaculate finish.

"Evening, Mr. Jacobey. You look nice yourself. Am I over or under-dressed?"

"Neither." He grinned and offered her his arm. "Shall we?"

Rebecca grabbed her purse, closed, and locked the door and allowed him to escort her to his vehicle. "May I ask where we're going?" she asked once they were on their way.

Ray smiled over at her. "The only casual place I could think of is usually crowded and that just wouldn't work for me, so I'm taking you someplace special."

"Really?"

He nodded. "Yep. It's a nice place. Quaint but cozy and I always get the best table in the house."

"I'm intrigued. Does it have a name?"

He laughed. "Ray's place."

A hint of unease curled in her stomach. "You're taking me to your house?"

"After the many times you've served me coffee or lunch I thought the least I could do was cook dinner for you." Ray glanced at her and must have noticed the apprehension in her eyes. He took her hand, raised it to his mouth, and pressed feathery kisses over her skin.

"You can trust me, Becca. I'd never do anything to hurt you."

The intimate gesture and the way he called her 'Becca' eased the pang of anxiety she felt. "I believe that, but your house...Seriously?" She arched an eyebrow in question.

He chuckled. "Don't worry. Though quiet and cozy, it's not very secluded. There are neighbors within hollering distance should you feel the need."

His teasing alleviated her worry. She smiled. "Well, just in case you get any weird ideas, my son knows I'll be with you this evening." She edged the words with laughter hoping to soften the sting of threat.

Ray laughed. "Point taken. How's he doing?"

"Fine, though he sounded a bit disgruntled when I said I was going out to dinner with you."

"Had he objected too strenuously, would you have changed your mind and not come?"

Rebecca shrugged. "I don't know. I never thought about

how my kids would feel should I ever start dating. I never thought that far ahead. I've just taken things one day at a time."

"Well, I'm glad you didn't have to make that choice." He pulled into the driveway of a small string of apartments. "Here we are."

Artfully arranged side-by-side, the building contained three apartments. Dark, redwood siding gave it a rustic look, which was complemented by a row of hedges separating the front of the building from the parking spaces. A brick pathway led to the doors and strategically placed flowering plants gave each tiny yard its own personality. A large porch and covered walkway provided a hint of protection from the elements and a white picket fence separated the property from neighboring houses.

Rebecca smiled over at Ray. "It's so pretty. I can't wait to see the rest."

He laughed, got out of the car, and walked around to open her door. Escorting her to his apartment, he unlocked the door and ushered her inside. Quaint and cozy described the beauty that surrounded her. Plush beige carpet covered the floor, wainscoting complemented the rustic look outside and a pretty country border added a touch of color to almond walls.

Stopping long enough to turn on some music, and then the oven, Raymond led her through the kitchen and opened the back door. Each apartment had its own patio. Separated with a partial six-foot privacy fence, they opened up to reveal a spacious yard.

"It's so sweet. Reminds me of some of the places we lived while Jim was in the Air Force."

dredge up the nerve.

Before she was ready, they had to call an end to the evening. A hushed awe filled the air when Ray drove her home, as though neither wanted to break the spell of such a lovely time with the word goodbye. Excitement warred with nerves the closer they got to her house. Having been out of the dating scene for so long—in actuality never having dated at all—Rebecca had no idea what Ray expected. Would he want to come in? Should she invite him? Would he want or expect to kiss her? Was she ready for that?

She knew her worries were unfounded when he pulled into her driveway and put the vehicle in park, then immediately disembarked and walked around to open her door. He held her hand all the way up on her porch, then took her key and unlocked the door.

"May I call you tomorrow?"

"Sure," she answered with a smile then gave him her number which he promptly programmed into his cell phone.

"Is this a landline or cell?"

"Landline. I hardly ever use my mobile."

Ray slid the device back into his pocket then clasped her hand once more and raised it to his lips. "Thank you for a lovely evening, Becca. I hope we can do it again soon."

Overwhelmed by his sweetness, Rebecca simply nodded and entered the house. She watched through the front door window as he walked back to his vehicle then drove away.

~*~

The next morning Rebecca fumbled for the phone as insistent ringing yanked her out of a sound sleep. "Hello?"

"Mom? Why didn't you call me when you got home last night? I left you a message to call no matter what time it was."

Rebecca awoke instantly at the frantic tone of her son's voice. "Oh, hi Jeff, it was late, and I didn't want to wake you."

"I don't care what time it was! You should have called."

Annoyance flared. Rebecca's eyebrow arched in the same motherly warning she'd used on her children from the time they were old enough to understand what it meant. "Excuse me, young man, but I am your mother. I do care what time it was, and I don't appreciate you using that tone with me."

Jeffrey huffed out a sigh, ground his teeth. "I'm sorry, Mother. I was worried. There are all sorts of psychos out there, and I don't even know this guy. Who is he anyway?"

Rebecca smiled at his use of "mother" instead of "mom"—a sure sign he was upset. "I appreciate your feelings on the matter, but I am a grown woman and perfectly capable of taking care of myself. However, his name is Raymond Jacobey, and he's been my mailman for nearly a year."

"He's the mailman, and she thinks she knows him well enough to stay out half the night."

He sounded so much like the disgruntled little boy he'd once been. Rebecca swallowed a giggle. "Did you say something?"

She imagined him scrubbing his hands over his face or raking them through his hair the way he always had when frustrated.

"No, Mom, not a thing. Just be careful will you? I don't want to lose you to some idiotic, deranged postal worker."

The giggle freed itself from her throat in a bubble of laughter. "You watch the news too much."

"And you don't watch it enough." The amusement in his voice lightened any sting in his words.

"If you're through fussing at me, may I ask when you're coming home?"

"We finish up on the twentieth of December. I'll fly out the twenty-first. When's Deb going to be there?"

"About the same time, I believe."

"Maybe we'll get together on the flight in."

Rebecca recognized loneliness in his voice and understood how much he missed his sister. "That would be nice. Why don't you give her a call and work it out."

"Hey, good idea. Why didn't I think of that?"

"Because you're too busy worrying about postal workers."

His laughter joined hers across the line.

"Are you taking care of yourself, eating right and getting enough sleep?"

"Yes, Ma'am," he said, still laughing.

A knock on her door interrupted further conversation. "Hang on, someone's knocking."

Rebecca laid the receiver on the bed, slid into her robe and slippers then went to see who was there. A young Asian man stood on the porch. She opened the door. "May I help you?"

"I'm looking for Jim Sinclair. Is he in?"

"No, he's not."

"Can you tell me when he'll be back?"

A surge of irritation hit Rebecca. "Look, I don't know who you are, but my husband's been dead for over a year."

She slammed the door shut on the kid's open-mouthed stare. Maybe she shouldn't have reacted so violently, but for months after Jim passed, a stream of people came or called.

People who should've known better. At least in her mind. Each time she had to tell someone Jim was gone it reopened the wound. She'd thought she'd never get to a place where she could utter his name and not disintegrate into pieces.

She made her way back into the bedroom and picked up the phone. "Are you still there?"

"Yes, I'm here."

"Now what were you saying?"

"Who was at the door?"

"Some kid looking for your father."

"What did he want?"

Rebecca frowned at the odd change in Jeff's tone.

"I don't know, probably to sell him something. I informed him that your father is deceased and closed the door on him. Why? What's wrong?"

"Nothing. Good for you." Jeff let out a deep breath. "Look, I gotta run. We'll talk again soon. Debbie or I will call you with the final details of our flights."

"OK. I love you, Jeff."

"Mom?"

"Yes?"

"Did you have a good time last night?"

She smiled into the receiver. "I had a lovely time. Thanks for asking."

"I'm glad. I love you. Take care and don't do anything I wouldn't do."

"I won't if you won't." Rebecca's heart ached at the familiar endearment she and Jim had used with both kids from the time they reached their early teens. Tears stung her eyes as she disconnected, but she blinked them back with determination.

Chapter Seven

Raymond picked up the phone and hesitated. He'd promised Rebecca he'd take it slow. *How slow is slow enough?*

He put on his robe, knotted the belt then slid into his slippers and went to make coffee. The moment he walked into the kitchen, memories of his evening with Becca thrummed through his senses. His heart trembled at the way the way her eyes sparkled when she smiled, her laugh, how good she felt in his arms when they danced. The number of things they had in common surprised him.

He put the kettle on to boil, rinsed the old-fashioned drip pot, and measured out fresh grounds for coffee. Thoughts of Rebecca continued to swirl through his mind. He'd be content to spend every night cooking her steak and dancing with her, listening to her talk. *Waking with her in his arms.* Odd thought, considering he'd yet to kiss her. Not very experienced in the art of romance or the ways of the flesh, he wondered how he should go about courting Rebecca before making her his wife. In that aspect, Ray realized he was totally out of his comfort zone, and in truth, way out of his league.

He would have to depend on more than his own strength to crawl out of his cave of shyness and insecurity. He'd have to depend on God to help him win Rebecca's heart. It hadn't been easy to summon the courage to ask her to dinner, asking her to marry him would be impossible. He'd have to compete with her memories of Jim, her children's needs, and feelings about him being involved in their lives, as well as her own fears and doubts. But he and Rebecca had crossed a milestone last night. The first of many, he hoped.

Now that their first date was out of the way, he wouldn't feel as pressured about making a good impression and getting everything right. Still, he wasn't sure what the next step should be. *It's certainly not sitting here waxing sentimental.*

Nor is it taking things too slowly.

That settled, he dialed her number.

"Hello?"

His heart skipped a beat at the sound of her voice. Ray smiled into the receiver. "Morning, Becca. Didn't wake you, did I?"

She laughed. "No, my son beat you to it. He called about an hour ago, mad as a hornet's nest that I didn't call him when I got home last night."

"Oh? Is he still angry?"

"No. I straightened him out real quick."

Ray chuckled. "Maybe you should call him next time, that way he'll know you're not out with some idiotic, deranged postal worker."

She giggled. "Those were his exact words."

"You're kidding."

She laughed again. "No."

"Are you afraid of that?" Ray asked, sobering his tone.

"Not a bit," she assured him.

"Good, got a question for you."

"Shoot."

He took a deep breath and plunged in. "What would you say if I reneged on my promise to take things slow between us?"

"What do you mean?"

"I mean that I want to get to know you as quickly and as intimately as possible."

"What?"

Strike one, he thought at the chill and shock in her tone. Ray groaned then took a deep breath. "I didn't mean that the way it sounded."

She remained silent.

"This is not the kind of conversation you have over the telephone. Meet me for breakfast?"

"I'm not sure it's the kind of conversation we should be having at all, much less in a crowded restaurant."

"You're right. But a crowded restaurant is better than someplace secluded and romantic. At least there you'll know I'm serious."

More silence from her end.

Ray's heart plummeted. *Lame, Ray, lame. Get back on track.* "So, will you meet me for breakfast?"

Rebecca's heart thudded. He'd told her his feelings went deeper than friendship, but he'd also said he wouldn't push. *Not* wanting to go slow sure felt like pushing, and she wasn't sure she was ready for anything more than friendship, even though she *had* enjoyed their date and the brief conversations they'd had over the past year as he delivered her daily mail.

She took a deep breath and sent up a short, silent prayer. Gut instinct told her Ray was a good man who wouldn't try to push her where she didn't want to go. "Yes, I'll meet you for breakfast."

An hour later, they arrived at the restaurant at the same time.

He took her hand and raised it to his mouth.

"Morning, Becca." He nuzzled her knuckles, then walked hand-in-hand with her into the restaurant.

"Just coffee for now," he told the waitress once they were seated. "Becca?"

"Coffee's fine."

They sat in awkward silence until coffee arrived then Ray enveloped her hand in his again. "Now, to clarify what I said. I didn't mean it to sound like I wanted to crawl into bed with you. Although that is a lovely prospect, I'm not that kind of guy. What I meant was, I don't want to rush you or scare you off, but neither do I want to purposely take things slow between us."

His eyes were warm and tender, his touch gentle. The calmness about him soothed her apprehension. Rebecca searched her heart and chose her words with care before answering. "Your friendship means the world to me."

She gave his hand a gentle squeeze. "Your sweet smile and charming personality have pulled me out of the pit of despair on more than one occasion, and I had a lovely time last night. But I'm not sure I'm ready for anything more than what we already share."

"But you're not opposed to the idea of a deeper relationship?"

"That depends on what you mean by deeper."

"What I mean is that I'd like to court you."

She bit back a smile. "Court?"

"Court or date, whatever they're calling it nowadays." A ruddy flush darkened his cheeks. "What I mean is that I want to spend as much time with you as I can. Not just my lunch hour, but evenings, days off, weekends. I want to go places with you, see things through your eyes. I...I want to get to know you, really get to know you. Not as the pretty widow on my route, but as Rebecca Sinclair. I want to know the things you like and the things you hate. I don't know how else to explain it, Becca, I'm not good with words."

The insecurity in his tone made her smile and eased her hesitancy. "I think you have a wonderful way with words. OK, we'll try it your way, but you have to promise not to get all huffy and sulk if I say we need to slow down or that I need some space."

He grinned. "I'm a grown man, grown men don't sulk."

"Ha! Don't even give me that, Raymond Jacobey. I was married for twenty-two years to a grown man, happen to be the mother of a twenty-one year old grown man, and I'll have you know that grown men are the biggest babies on the planet. Don't leer at me either," she added. "You know exactly what I mean. Don't get your way and you pout, get angry and you sulk. And heaven forbid if you don't feel well, then you're worse than a room full of cranky two-year-olds."

He chuckled. "That's because God created us to be the strong ones, the provider and protector, and when we're not able to fulfill that role, it throws us all out of kilter. But whatever, I promise not to sulk or pout if you tell me to back off."

"OK, Ray, I'll let you set the pace, but let's take this relationship one step at a time."

He laughed. "Great. Last night was step one, step two,

breakfast." He signaled the waitress for menus.

Breakfast was romantic and sweet and not at all awkward.

When it was over, Ray snatched up the ticket, paid their tab, and then walked with her out to her car. "So, what do you have planned for today?"

Rebecca shrugged. "Haven't a clue. Since I cleaned and scrubbed and waxed the kitchen and utility room the other day, I thought that I'd move on to clean another room. The house could definitely use an overall scrubbing. It has never gone this long without one."

"Spend the day with me, we'll take a drive."

Rebecca hesitated. She wasn't sure if spending the day together would be too much too soon.

"C'mon. If the house has gone this long without a thorough scrubbing, one more day won't hurt. Besides, weather like this won't hold out much longer," he coaxed with a smile.

He was right. Though chilly, the beautiful morning held the promise of an even lovelier day. The sun continued in its rise, full and glowing. Not a single dark cloud marred the brilliant blue sky. But that could change in an instant when one lived so close to mountains and volcanoes.

She nodded in agreement and let him lead her to his SUV.

He pulled out of the parking lot and headed south.

"Where are we going?"

"To Paradise," he said with a wink and a grin.

Rebecca smiled back and settled in for the two-hour drive to Paradise Point—one of the highest peaks accessible by vehicle on Mt. Rainer. Those who wished to go higher than the Paradise Inn had to hike.

As Ray began to navigate the long, winding road upward, Rebecca couldn't help but remember her dream from a few nights ago and the letter she'd received.

Closing her eyes, she tried to recall every detail. This drive was surrounded by banks of snow as high as eight feet, interspersed with splashes of waterfalls cascading onto the road, but the drive in her dream was much different...the long, winding road, the glint of silver in her rear-view mirror, the smell of grapes in the air, the sight of dark, green shrubs overloaded with lilacs...she shook her head with a sigh.

Ray glanced at her. "Tired?"

"No, confused."

He frowned. "About what?"

"I can't get that crazy dream out of my head, or that stupid letter."

Ray shot her a glance. "I take it you haven't decided to read it yet, even after our conversation last night."

"No, I haven't."

He chuckled. "And I take it by your tone of voice I'd better not ask why."

Rebecca smiled at his teasing. "You can ask all you want, but don't expect an answer."

"You're not the least bit curious?"

"Oh, I'm sure there's a bit of morbid curiosity in here somewhere," she answered, pointing to her head.

He arched an eyebrow at her. "But?"

"But it's buried beneath the fear, anger and bitterness in here." She placed her hand over her heart.

Ray reached over, took her hand in his, and kissed it. "Don't worry over it so much, Becca, it'll come. It's waited thirty-some-odd years. It can wait a little longer. One morning, you'll open your eyes and your heart and read the letter. Hopefully, it'll all make sense when you do. Who knows, you might even find some answers and possibly a sense of peace about the whole situation."

She sighed. "I sure hope so."

A minute later, he pulled into a parking spot at Paradise Point. When he opened his door and climbed out of the vehicle, she shivered. "Ooohhh, I didn't think of how chilly it would be up here compared to at home."

Ray reached over the seat and pulled out a jacket for each of them.

"You thought to bring jackets? You must have had this planned."

He chuckled. "Wish I could take credit for being so ingenious, but they're here because I've found I usually need one at the oddest of times, and then I forget to take it in when I get home." He helped her into the warmer of the two. "Take a walk?"

Rebecca looked down at her blue jeans and tennis shoes. "I'm not really dressed for hiking."

"Me neither, but we can walk anyway. We won't go far, and then I'll buy you a cup of hot chocolate."

Rebecca let him lead her up the snow-covered bank until they stood in a clearing looking out to where heaven and earth met in a glorious profusion of rock and sky. Clouds surrounded mountain peaks like halos. A rainbow shimmered in the sky, brilliant colors against a backdrop of aqua so breathtaking they literally gasped for air.

Awe filled her so much she whispered, "It's so beautiful."

Ray slid his arms around her waist, and she leaned

against his chest. He rested his chin on her head, and they stood in silence gazing at the raw beauty of creation until the damp chill permeated their clothes.

Ray ran his hands down her arms, took Rebecca's hands in his, and then turned her to face him. She could see his heart in his eyes.

"'The earth declares the glory of the Lord; the heavens proclaim His handiwork.' That might not be an exact quote, but close enough. It is beautiful. Thank you for sharing it with me."

Rebecca's heart fluttered at the charming, boyish grin he bestowed on her. She knew he'd spoken more than mere words. He'd spoken his heart. Tears filled her eyes and clogged her throat when she thought about what the future might hold. Standing on the threshold of that great unknown, she had never been more acutely aware of anything than she was of this moment, this man.

He looked at her intently. His thumbs stroked the back of her hands, chasing the chill from her blood. Lethargic warmth stole over her. As though in a fog, she watched him lift her hands to his mouth and press his lips to her palm in a touch so tender it sent shivers down her spine.

He lifted her chin and waited until she looked at him again. "I want to kiss you, Becca, here in the midst of Paradise." He moved slowly. His lips hovered a moment then covered hers with devastating tenderness.

He let out a primitive grunt of satisfaction as he let go of her hands and pulled her closer. An answering purr escaped her as tiny pinpoints of pleasure bathed her senses with light and color. Never in her life had she felt so alive, so consumed with sensations.

Whether a moment or an eternity, she had no idea how long they stood there, his mouth in sweet possession of hers, but when the kiss was over, she realized she was plastered against his hard body. Her breathing came in sharp, almost painful rasps, and her fingers were clenched in his thick, sandy-colored hair. Appalled at her wanton response and the needy way in which she clung, Rebecca stumbled away with a startled cry of distress, and began to run.

Chapter Eight

Ray stood, stunned into immobility by the way Rebecca shoved herself out of his arms. "Rebecca, wait!"

She stumbled through the snow, sobbing then tripped, spurring him into action.

"Rebecca, please. Stop." His breath came in ragged pants as he hurried to catch her.

Boulders and small stones cluttered the path. Slippery patches of ice covered by snow gave way beneath his feet as he raced after her. "God, help me," he muttered, realizing the danger she was in.

On a sudden rush of adrenaline, he grabbed at her and missed. Lunging forward he tried again, this time snagging her by the jacket. "For heaven's sake, Rebecca, slow down, you're close to the edge."

His arm snaked around her waist as they tumbled to the ground. Using the weight of his body, he took advantage of the momentum and rolled them backward, down the incline and away from the precipice.

"Are you all right?" he asked when they came to a halt.

She wasn't sobbing now, but calm. Frighteningly so. She lifted wide, terrified eyes to his. "You're wrong, Ray. I've been teetering on the edge for more than a year now."

The ache in her voice stabbed his heart. "Somehow, I doubt we're talking about the same edge." He picked up a handful of snow, packed it into a firm ball and tossed it to where it disappeared into thin air a mere few feet from where they lay.

A horrified gasp escaped her. Rebecca scrambled into a sitting position and scooted further back.

Rolling to his feet, Ray offered her a hand up. "C'mon, let's get out of this snow."

Rebecca's hand trembled as she placed it in his. Once she'd gained her feet, Raymond took her gently but firmly by the arm and led her back down the mountain. A tense silence accompanied them to the vehicle. There was no lighthearted banter, no teasing flirtations, and no offer of the hot chocolate he'd promised earlier.

Rebecca's eyes were swollen with tears, and she looked terrified.

Ray opened the passenger door and helped her in without saying a word. Crossing behind the vehicle, he took a couple of deep breaths to calm his raging senses. His mind whirled in shock at what had happened, adrenaline pumped through his veins so fast he could hardly breathe.

Fear of rejection gnawed at his heart assisted by the jagged teeth of insecurity. His stomach churned with anxiety combined with the thick bile of uncertainty, all coated with guilt.

He climbed in beside her and started the car, letting the engine run a few minutes before backing out of the parking lot. Within moments, the vehicle was heated to toasty perfection, but the chill in his heart hadn't even begun to thaw.

Rebecca stared out the window, appearing numb to everything around her.

He could almost see her trembling. He forced his eyes back to the road. "You want to tell me what happened back there?"

Rebecca glanced over then looked away. "I've never been so humiliated in my life."

The temper he rarely displayed bubbled to surface. *Humiliated? She was humiliated? Why of all the unmitigated gall! Had he put his hands on her inappropriately, maybe he could understand her sentiments....* Ray cleared his throat and ground his teeth in order to bite back the angry retorts that sprang to mind. "I beg your pardon. You want to explain that one?"

Her smile was self-mocking. "Oh, please, Ray. Another few minutes of that and you'd have known me as intimately as a man could. Right there on the ground."

Ray saw red. Bright, hot, furious red. He pulled into one of the many roadside viewing areas along the mountain, ground the vehicle to a slamming halt and faced her.

"Do you think I'd take advantage of you like that? Do you honestly believe I'm so insensitive? I'll admit that it didn't do my ego a bit of harm to feel the sweetness of your response. But don't you think I recognize the fact that you haven't been kissed in over a year and that it was a mixture of pleasure and loneliness? Do you really think I'm so shallow as to not understand?"

If Rebecca was stunned by her response to Ray's kiss, she was doubly so at his reaction now. She watched in shocked silence as his laughing green eyes flashed, his sweet smile drew into a frown. His charming countenance shifted, a kaleidoscope of emotions flitted across his features...frustration rode on the heels of anger followed quickly by insecurity and pain.

Her heart clenched as realization hit. She'd hurt him. Not his pride, but his feelings, and that was unacceptable. With trembling fingers, she pried one of his hands off the steering wheel. It lay like a dead weight in her grasp when he held himself rigid, aloof.

She could feel the pain radiating from him. Deep. Raw. She swallowed the knot in her throat. "No. I'd never think that of you. It's not you. It's me. I've...," her voice trailed off, astounded by her next thought, shaken at what she'd almost said... *I've never been kissed like that.*

"You've what?"

Avoiding his gaze, Rebecca raised a trembling hand to rub at her temple. "I don't know how to explain what it is I'm trying to say."

"Just say it, Rebecca. You've what?"

She couldn't. To admit another man had made her feel things Jim never did would betray her husband and the love they'd shared. She shook her head. "I don't *know* what it is I'm trying to say."

Her gaze lifted to his, searching for understanding while her mind tried to come up with an explanation that would appease them both. "I'm sorry. I didn't intend to make you angry or hurt your feelings. You said you wanted to get to know me. Not as the widow on your route, but the real me. The real Rebecca Sinclair. I'm not sure even I know who she is. I've always been Rebecca Sinclair, wife of Jim Sinclair, mother of Jeffrey and Debbie Sinclair. That's who I am."

Ray shook his head. "That's what you are, not who. You are—or were—a wife, and you will always be a mother, but that's only a part of who you are." His grip tightened in hers, his voice softened and reassured her. "I want to know the woman beneath the labels." He shook his head again. "And I'm sorry if I lost it there for a minute."

He looked into her eyes, and the affection reflected there made her heart race.

"I like you a lot, Becca, and I care about you. Your words took me by surprise—to think that you could even consider...but I guess you really don't know me, do you?" He looked away, out the windshield to a sky filled with burgeoning colors.

She squeezed his hand and drew his attention back to her. "I do know you, Ray. You are kind and supportive, and you're a wonderful friend. You're sweet and romantic."

Bubbles of heat burst beneath her skin. A self-conscious giggle escaped her tense lips. "I- I'm out of practice with all that. Not that I ever had a lot of practice to begin with. Jim and I knew each other forever and married so young. We didn't do a lot of flirting. Or dating for that matter. We just..."

She shrugged. "Were... For lack of a better word. Always together, always a couple and then a family."

"So, you're not angry with me? Or frightened?"

Rebecca shook her head. "No."

Tension dissipated. His smile returned. He squeezed her hand then lifted it and kissed the palm. "Good."

Relief curled through Rebecca. She still had her self-respect, her dignity. And she still had his friendship. She cupped his cheek. "Your friendship means the world to me, Ray. I never want to lose it."

"You won't."

"I don't even know where to start in finding out who Rebecca Sinclair is."

"Perhaps we can discover her together," Ray said his tone gentle. "I know I've asked you this before, but have you thought about going to school or getting a job?"

"Not really. Whenever I think about those things, or try to think about them, the same questions come to mind...go to school for what? Get a job doing what? Like I've said before, I have no skills outside of being a wife and mother and no education outside of a G.E.D."

Ray shook his head. "You're limiting yourself and your abilities by thinking like that. There's a lot more involved in being a wife and mother than you're taking into consideration; housekeeper, bookkeeper, nurse, child care expert, chef...you have to think outside the box, Rebecca."

"Maybe so," she said. "But what does thinking outside the box do for me in terms of furthering my education or getting a job?"

"Well, how about a child care attendant in a nursery or day care, a cashier, or a restaurant hostess. Many of those positions don't require more than a high school diploma. As for school, I'm not sure. What are your interests and hobbies?"

Rebecca smiled. "Hobbies? My youngest child just graduated from high school and left home. Up until now, there hasn't been time for hobbies. I mean, I did all the things a wife and mother does: cook, clean, bake, sew. And I enjoyed them all, but other than reading, I don't have any hobbies."

He shrugged. "Well maybe it's time for you to get some. Volunteer at a hospital or nursing home or something. Get out of the house and meet people. Find your passion and set goals for yourself."

"Find my passion? You sound like one of those self-help gurus on TV."

He chuckled. "Guess I could do a lot worse. They do have a point though."

A tap on the driver's window of the vehicle interrupted further conversation. Ray rolled down the window.

"Everything OK in there?" A policeman asked.

"Yes, Sir." Ray nodded in assurance.

"Ma'am?"

Rebecca leaned forward with a smile. "Yes. We're just talking."

The patrolman nodded. "OK, but it's time to move on. A storm's brewing. We're advising everyone to get off the mountain."

"No problem." Ray rolled up the window, put the vehicle in gear, and then maneuvered back onto the roadway and headed down the mountain once more. He glanced in the rearview mirror. "Look back, Becca. Isn't it amazing how quickly darkness can slither in, covering the light and hiding its beauty?"

She twisted in her seat and looked at the mountain. Dark thunderclouds had moved in, shrouding the splendorous peaks.

His words sank deep. Rebecca felt the sharp stab of them. *Just like when we kissed.* Though he hadn't said it aloud, the thought reverberated and cut to the heart. Hers twisted with guilt. Taking his hand once more, she brought it to her cheek. "I'm so sorry, Ray. I didn't mean to spoil the beauty of your kiss."

His smile was tender. "And I didn't mean to insinuate that." He tugged their hands to his mouth, pressed a kiss to the fingertips and gave her hand a gentle squeeze. "Let's forget it, OK?"

"Thank you," she whispered, blinking back tears.

The ride back to the restaurant was in companionable silence, interspersed with snatches of conversation. Rebecca thought about all that had transpired between them. He'd given her a lot to think about, a lot to pray about. Emotional outbursts were not the norm for her, and she was relieved to finally get in her car and head home.

That evening, unable to sleep, Rebecca roamed the house. All afternoon and evening, she'd wrestled with demons over the incident with Ray. Many times, she'd picked up the phone wanting to be reassured of his continued friendship—that she hadn't hurt him too deeply—but had never called him, afraid of what he might say after having time to think things over.

Memories of his kiss tortured her body and haunted her mind. *I've never been kissed like that.* The realization was like a dousing of cold water, numbing her heart with the truth. No, it couldn't be true! She'd been married for twenty-two years to a wonderful man. Surely she'd felt that before.

Rebecca closed her eyes and tried to recall how it felt to be in Jim's arms, his lips gently caressing hers. Pleasure, soft, sweet, and tender was all she could remember ever feeling with him.

A groan of frustration rose. Tears filled her eyes. Rebecca raked her fingers through her hair and then pressed the heels of her hands over her eyes before burying her face in the palms. "God please help me to understand what I'm feeling."

Her musings from a couple of nights ago played themselves over in her mind. This time, sadness filled her instead of longing. She realized that no matter how much she wanted to believe otherwise, hot bubble baths and full-body massages with scented oil followed by exquisite lovemaking were not the norm for her and Jim.

Even though they'd had a satisfying relationship, she'd reached the pinnacle of passion she'd imagined only a handful of times in all their years of marriage. Though she'd enjoyed her husband's kiss, it was nothing like the soul-jarring thrill she experienced in Ray's arms.

Picking up her mail, she glanced through it and then dropped it on the table without opening a single envelope. *No scented stickers on this packet.*

Plopping into a chair, she buried her head on her arms and let the tears come, as guilt rose to torment her once more. She reached for the phone, desperately wanting someone to talk to. But who? One of the kids? She shook her head, they'd never understand. She picked up the yellow-pages directory and thumbed through it, not sure exactly what she was looking for.

A twenty-four hour counseling hotline number jumped out at her. She hesitated.

Jim would never have allowed her to talk about their problems to a stranger. His voice rose in her mind. "You'll not put our business on the street."

She shook her head, shocked—surprised even—that his voice would rise up now to chide her when it hadn't bothered to offer a single word of comfort over the past year.

"It's not your business anymore," she said aloud. Anger set in, spewed forth in her next words. "You're dead and I'm here all by myself. How could you do this to me, Jim Sinclair, knowing the kids' dreams would take them so far away? How could you leave me to face the rest of my life alone? I don't even have a headstone to visit."

She pushed out of the chair to pace the kitchen, giving vent to the fury coursing through her. "You, with your grand ideas of being cremated and your ashes thrown out of an airplane, have left me totally alone! And now, when I really need someone to talk to, someone who'll listen to *my* feelings, you decide to speak up. How dare you?"

She dialed the number. Before she could hang up, a gentle, reassuring voice came on the line.

"Hello, Christian Counseling Service, how may I help you?"

Words tumbled from her mouth of their own accord. Rebecca told all, every feeling, every detail of the past year even up to the incident with Ray that afternoon. Emotionally spent, she slumped into the chair and rested her head on her arm while the phone, held limply against her ear, dangled precariously in her fingers.

"Are you still there?" The quiet voice asked.

"Yes." Rebecca had never realized how much energy uttering a single syllable could take.

"Good. Let me begin by saying that everything you're feeling right now is perfectly normal. I've been a counselor for many years, and if there's one thing I've learned, it's that grief is multifaceted. Your friend is right, it's time for you to start moving forward with your life, and I agree with him about the letter. Give yourself time to assimilate your feelings before you open it. After more than thirty years, another few weeks or so won't hurt."

There was a brief pause of the gentle voice. "I believe God is calling you out of your circumstances, the normality of life as you have known it. If I may, I suggest you find a church family. Don't be in a rush about it but visit those around you. Let God lead you to the place where He wants you to be. Until you do, there are many great ministers on television who can help to guide you."

"Jim never liked churches. Nor did he respect TV preachers."

"May I ask why?"

"I'm not sure, exactly. He just never could get comfortable in places of what he termed as formal, structured religion, and he said TV preachers were phonies who were only after your money. We always read our Bible and prayed, and we raised our kids up in the way of the Lord. He allowed them to visit their friends' churches whenever they wanted, but we never found one he was comfortable with."

"How do you feel about it?"

Rebecca thought for a moment, considered her answer carefully, prayerfully. "There were a couple of places over the years that I liked, but I tried to be respectful of my husband and his opinions. Isn't that what a good wife should do?"

The counselor was quiet, and Rebecca assumed he also was prayerfully considering his response.

"I don't think any man should have that much control over a woman's thoughts and feelings, even if she is his wife. There is a balance to the 'women respect your husbands' directive that doesn't involve following blindly. But I'm not here to judge your beliefs, your husband, or your convictions. If you believed in your heart you were doing God's will, then it's OK. But that time of your life is over. It's time for you to start thinking and feeling for yourself. It's OK not to concern yourself with your husband's way of thinking. It's time to grow into the woman God wants you to be."

"But how do I do that? Where do I start?"

"What translation of the Bible do you have?"

"We have a couple of different ones around here. Jim was very into God's Word, and he studied it faithfully."

"Sounds like he was a man after God's heart."

"He was gentle and kind and respectful. He believed wholly in the Bible and sought to understand it and God."

"That's good. Please forgive me if I've insinuated otherwise. I believe he was, as you say, a good man. But I also believe it's time for you to stand up and be counted for who you are as an individual. You were a good and faithful wife, but now it's time to move beyond those things and become the woman God wants you to be in this new chapter of your life."

"Everyone keeps saying that, but no one will tell me what to do or where to start." Her voice quivered. Fresh tears welled in her eyes and throat.

The counselor prayed aloud asking the Holy Spirit for wisdom and guidance. "OK, here's what I think you should do. Get a women's devotional Bible. There are many good editions out there. Go to the bookstore, browse through them all and pick the one you feel God is leading you to buy. Then, start visiting area churches. Don't feel you have to mix and mingle with all of the people right away but do linger and talk to those who approach you. God will put people in your path to help, to give you words of wisdom, guidance, and direction. So be open to those who approach you.

"You might want to ask about and consider joining a Bible study group or something like it. Another good idea is

Chapter Nine

Rebecca walked onto the porch, reached for her mail, and felt a tug of disappointment that she'd missed Ray.

When she'd left the house earlier, she had every intention of being home in time to see him. Taking the advice of the counselor, she'd headed to the nearest bookstore first thing this morning. She purchased a cup of coffee in the store café and wandered to the "Inspirational" section only to be overwhelmed by the variety of Bibles there. After picking those that seemed to be geared especially for women, she found a comfortable chair and glanced through each edition. All were lovely, touching, but only one caused her spirit to quicken.

She'd held on to it and put the others back then browsed through the assortment of inspirational books available and picked out a few. If her only hobby was reading, she might as well make the most of it by reading something uplifting, something that might help give wisdom and direction for her life.

Now she was anxious to get inside and get started. She dropped the mail into the bag along with her purchases, got a whiff of scent and smiled. He'd given her roses this time.

Once inside, she emptied the contents of the bag, picked up the packet of envelopes and sorted through them, putting the bills aside and throwing away the junk. Attached to the last envelope with a round smiley-face sticker. Ray's note made her giggle.

I was here and you were gone, now you're here and I

am gone. And hungry. Guess I'll have to settle for a cold burger in an impersonal atmosphere, instead of fresh sandwiches in the presence of your lovely company. He'd drawn a frown. *Talk to you soon. Have a blessed day. Hugs, Ray.*

Rebecca peeled the smiley face off the envelope and stuck the note to the refrigerator where she would be reminded of his kindness and continued friendship, vowing to pray for him every time she saw it.

Her stomach grumbled, telling her it was way past lunch, and she hadn't eaten breakfast. She fixed herself a sandwich, ate, then settled into her favorite chair and opened her new Bible.

Edited by a popular minister, the book was filled with inspirational articles, nuggets of gold and pearls of wisdom all specifically designed with the sole purpose of offering healing and restoration to a woman's spirit.

Though she'd read the Scriptures many times before, Rebecca found that the added words of hope and healing—all based on the minister's unique comprehension of the Bible—brought a fresh perspective to the depth and power of God's love and compassion. She found herself skimming through the pages anxious to read the next article, excited about God's Word in ways she'd never experienced before.

She didn't realize how long she sat or how much she'd read until someone knocked on her door. She put the Bible on the table and glanced at the clock, surprised to note that it was nearly five o'clock in the evening.

She glanced out the door, and then swung it open on a surge of irritation. "I thought I made myself clear the last time you showed up," she said to the Asian boy who had knocked on her door a few days ago.

His complexion reddened. Remorse curdled her stomach when he took a step back and shoved his hands in his pockets.

"Sorry, ma'am, I don't mean to bother. Only a moment of your time, please." His shoulders hunched in a defeated slump when she didn't answer.

Rebecca sighed. It wasn't in her nature to be rude. "What can I do for you?"

He looked up at her with dark, earnest eyes. "Your husband, when he die?"

"Over a year ago."

"I sorry."

"Thank you. Is that all?"

"May I ask a few questions about him?"

Rebecca studied him a moment before answering. Lean and long-limbed, he appeared to be around eighteen or nineteen years old. Though dressed like any other teenager in jeans and a sweater, the dark hair, olive complexion and almond-shaped eyes revealed his heritage. Something about the shadow of pain and the hint of fear in his gaze tugged at her heart.

"How do you know my husband?"

Unease crawled up her spine when he hesitated, seemed to search for words.

"Your husband was in Air Force, right?"

More statement than question Rebecca nodded, wondering how this kid could know that.

"He stationed in Korea?"

A knot of apprehension formed at the base of her skull. "A couple of times."

He smiled. "He kind to my mother. She encourage me to look him up when I come to school in United States. I sorry to hear about his death."

Shamed now by her previous treatment of him, Rebecca stepped away from the door. "Would you like to come in?"

Surprise registered on his face, followed by joy. His quick grin touched her in a way only a mother would understand.

"Thank you."

The phone rang, interrupting their conversation. Excusing herself, she left the young man to follow or wait, and raced to the kitchen to answer it. "Hello?"

"Rebecca?"

Ray's voice, raw and fierce, sent a shiver of concern down her spine. "Ray? What's wrong?"

"I just got a call. My parents were killed in a car wreck earlier this evening."

"Oh, no, I'm so sorry."

"I have to go to Flagstaff."

"Of course, you do."

"I..." his voice broke. "I don't want to. I hate that place. But no matter how mixed up they were or how lonely my childhood, they're still my parents."

"You're right."

"Come with me, Becca."

The request startled her. "What?"

"Come with me. We'll take a late flight out and be there in a few hours."

"But..."

"Please, Rebecca. I'm not sure I can do this alone."

In light of all the times he'd been there for her in the past year, she could not in all good conscience, refuse him now.

"OK, Ray. Give me time to pack a suitcase. How long will we be gone?"

A heavy breath sounded through the line.

"Thank you. We'll only be gone for a day or two.

"Where will we, or more specifically where will I, stay?"

"It's a huge house, there's plenty of room. But if you're not comfortable with that, I'll put you up at a hotel. We have plenty of time to decide on the flight in."

Rebecca murmured noncommittally, unsure of the propriety of staying in the same house with a single man—and one she barely knew if she were completely honest.

"Call your kids, Becca. At least one of them and let them know what's going on. Don't want Jeffery to think I've abducted you or anything like that."

Though it wavered, Rebecca heard the smile in his voice. She promised to do so and to be ready by the time he got there to pick her up.

She hung up and returned to her guest, who'd waited politely in the foyer. She offered an apologetic smile. "I'm sorry. You'll have to come back another time. A friend has an emergency." She opened the door for him to leave.

The young man obeyed without the slightest hesitation.

He was long gone before Rebecca realized she'd never even asked his name. After packing her suitcase, Rebecca glanced at her watch and figured she might be able to talk to both of her children before Ray arrived.

Debbie was her usual sweet self, accepting without question why Rebecca felt the need to go with Ray.

Jeffery wasn't so understanding. "How well do you know this guy?"

Rebecca heard the real question in her son's voice.

"Not as well as you might be imagining. Have you forgotten how I raised you, Jeff, or do you just think I have?"

"No, Mom. I wasn't thinking that at all."

But Rebecca heard the hint of guilt in his voice that convinced her he had at least considered the thought that she and Ray were intimate already.

"Your sister didn't seem to have a problem with my going."

He snorted. "I can imagine she didn't. She's too naive and trusting. Just like you. And she thinks he's 'incredibly sweet and cute'. At least I think those were her words when I spoke with her the other day."

Rebecca smiled at the hint of annoyance in her son's voice. "He is both of those things. He's also charming, gentle, kind, and unless I'm mistaken, very much in love with me." She knew it was true the moment the words left her mouth, and she wondered how her son would feel about that.

Jeff remained silent.

"He's been a wonderful friend to me this past year, and I can't—let me rephrase that—I *won't* let him down now, when he needs me to be the same for him."

Jeff heaved a sigh.

Rebecca imagined him rubbing his forehead the way he did when he was frustrated or upset. "Don't you trust my judgment? Or at least trust me enough to know my own heart and mind."

"Of course, I do. It's just that I don't know this guy, and I don't want to see you get hurt. Promise you'll call me while you're with him, Mom. At least once or twice while you're there and when you get home, so I'll know you're OK."

Rebecca agreed.

They talked for a few more minutes, their conversation ending when Ray arrived.

The flight was quiet, uneventful. Rebecca told Ray of her conversation with the counselor and her subsequent visit to the bookstore.

"I wouldn't have minded you calling me, Becca."

She smiled tenderly and took his hand. "I know, but I've always heard that sometimes it's easier to talk to a stranger."

Rebecca noted the tired, strained expression on his face and refrained from further conversation. She gave his hand a reassuring squeeze and said a silent prayer for his emotional wellbeing when he put his seat into a reclining position and closed his eyes.

They sat in companionable silence for the remainder of the flight, but as the pilot began his descent into Flagstaff, Rebecca actually felt the tension building in Ray. His grip on her hand tightened, his shoulders stiffened, he put his seat up with a forceful snap, and once they landed, he wasn't in a hurry to gather their things and get off the plane.

After the last person had passed his seat, Ray let go of Rebecca's hand and rose. Stepping back, he allowed her into the aisle before reaching into the overhead compartment to retrieve their carry-on bags.

The time it took to deplane and rent a car did very little to ease the palpable tension. His unease made Rebecca increasingly more uncomfortable, and she silently reminded herself that she was present to support him, and that her own feelings were not a priority.

Once out of the airport, Ray asked Rebecca what she wanted to do about sleeping arrangements.

Rebecca hesitated only a moment before answering. The

Bible instructed believers to avoid the appearance of sin, but it also said a true friend sticks closer than a brother. She reached for his hand. "I'll stay at your parents' home, but in a different room."

"It's not a home, it's a mausoleum. A home is built on love, joy, and happiness, none of that existed in this place."

The harshness of his voice surprised her.

He emitted a strained, bitter little laugh. "Maybe we should both stay in a hotel."

Rebecca's heart broke at the pain and resentment in his voice. "Whatever you think is best, Ray, I'm here for you."

"And that's what friends are for, right?"

Rebecca winced at the underlying edge to his voice. He may have forgiven her, but he hadn't forgotten. She raised his hand to her cheek, rubbed it against her skin then brushed her lips across it as he had done numerous times to her.

Ray sighed, tugging their joined hands to his lips. "I'm sorry, Becca. I don't mean to take my feelings out on you."

Rebecca pulled her hand from his grasp and stroked his cheek with her fingers. "It's OK. That's what friends are for."

The tension in his face prevented a smile from forming on his lips or reaching his eyes. "Touché. I'm grateful you came, Becca. I may not show it over the next few days, but please know that I am."

Darkness shrouded the mountain peaks north of the city as they drove the five miles from the airport into Flagstaff. Lights twinkled in the distance and although the silence between them wasn't unbearable, neither was it comfortable. The agitation emanating from Ray clouded the atmosphere like a dense fog. Rebecca wondered what kind of emotional upheaval awaited him over the next few days.

He rolled into the driveway of a huge, two-story house. "Well, here we are."

Red brick with white pillars, the house looked as though it belonged on a luxurious estate instead of a small, crowded, city block.

Rebecca thought the structure beautiful, but she could understand how a frustrated young boy could consider it big, cold, and lonely—especially if his parents were largely absent.

Chapter Ten

Ray fished a set of keys out of his pocket. He pressed the button necessary to disengage the security system, then another to unlock and release the automatic garage door. Lights came on as it opened. He drove the car inside, parked, and then got out to open Rebecca's door. Offering his hand, he resisted the urge to pull her in his arms and cover her lips with his.

When he kissed her again, it would be on her terms. Besides, he couldn't risk another rejection right now. If he kissed her and she bolted as before, he might not survive the betrayal.

As though reading his thoughts, Rebecca smiled and then brushed her lips across his in a tender caress. "I'm sorry I hurt you yesterday, Ray, I promise to try and not do it again."

Oh, how he wanted to hold her. Instead, Ray whispered his thanks and gave her hand a gentle squeeze before releasing it. Giving her the keys, he showed her which one opened the door to the house then went to the trunk of the car to retrieve their luggage. Once inside, he led her to the guest room nearest his bedroom, then back down into the kitchen. "Are you hungry?" he asked, rummaging through the refrigerator.

Rebecca nodded.

Together, they prepared a quick meal of soup and sandwiches, ate in companionable silence, then cleaned the kitchen together.

Ray showed her to her bedroom door, pressed a light kiss

to her forehead, and then reluctantly went to his own room. He understood and agreed that they shouldn't stay in the same room, but the desire to hold Rebecca in his arms threatened to consume his common sense. Something inside him felt that her nearness could ease his bitterness and grief, and he needed that right now. Comfort. Companionship. Hope.

He changed into pajamas and climbed into bed. The cold sheets stole his body heat. Sleep didn't come at first, but when it finally eased through his mind, his dreams were filled with disquiet, and nothing tangible he could hold on to.

~*~

Rebecca awoke early the next morning, made her way down the stairs and into the kitchen where she found a note from Ray saying that he'd gone to check on funeral arrangements for his parents.

She wondered if he'd thought about food and refreshments to offer the guests who were bound to pour into the house throughout the day. Figuring he hadn't, she did a thorough search of the refrigerator, freezer, and pantry, making a mental list of things she could put together.

The door rattled and she looked up from perusing the contents of the refrigerator.

"What'cha looking for?"

Rebecca smiled. "Good morning. What did you find out?"

"Everything's all set. There'll be a memorial service this afternoon. Evidently, my parents discussed everything with their attorney, even the funeral. He made the arrangements yesterday afternoon. So, what are you looking for?"

"I'm taking stock of what's available in terms of providing food for the guests I'm sure you'll be having."

"Don't go to any trouble. I thought I'd call a catering service for that."

"It's no trouble. It's what I do best, remember? Or is holding your hand the only reason you brought me here?"

Ray chuckled and reached for her hand. "I'm at my best when you're holding my hand, Becca. And it's such a lovely hand to hold onto." He raised the appendage to his mouth, kissed it.

Rebecca's cheeks warmed. "You are an incurable flirt, Raymond Jacobey."

"Scott."

"What?"

"My middle name is Scott. If you're going to address me by my given name you should know that. "You know, when you want to be sure I listen." He frowned with mock ferocity. "Raymond Scott Jacoby," he growled as if he meant business.

Rebecca laughed. "I'll remember that from now on. How about some breakfast?"

"I thought we'd go out for breakfast."

Rebecca shook her head. "Go out for breakfast and hire a caterer to provide for your guests? Sounds cold and impersonal to me."

"Breakfast with you would never be cold or impersonal. As for the other, they're only people passing through. I don't know them. They will be my parents' friends. My parents would think a caterer would be more than adequate in providing them with what they're accustomed to being served."

Rebecca flinched inwardly at the coldness of his voice

and wondered if he would ever find anything good to remember about his parents. Twenty-two years of marriage had taught her to compromise. Maybe too much. Both Raymond and the counselor had insisted she start thinking and acting for herself, so she ignored the tendency to comply this time.

"Well, I think it's rude, Mr. Raymond *Scott* Jacobey. You asked me to come along for support, so allow me to do that in the way I know best. This kitchen is exceptionally stocked and it's a shame to let it all go to waste. Now, what would you like for breakfast?"

Ray answered her question, accepted the breakfast she laid out before him, and then got out of her way so she could prepare food for the people who would soon be trailing in and out of the house.

By the time they got ready to leave for the memorial service, Rebecca hoped she had prepared enough to feed everyone who showed up. She surveyed the food spread on the huge table in the formal dining room. There were finger sandwiches made of tuna, chicken and ham salad, fruit with cream cheese dip, vegetables with ranch dip and two trays filled with homemade cookies, brownies, and fudge. A large crystal bowl held punch made of white grape juice and ginger ale. More of the same chilled in the refrigerator. The coffee pot was ready and set to begin brewing in an hour. Cups, saucers, and napkins were laid out, as were silverware and plates.

Ray stepped up beside her and examined the feast. He whistled and slipped his arm around her waist. "Everything looks wonderful."

She smiled at him. "I think I've found my passion.

Though I have no idea where it'll lead me."

His smile, though strained, was tender. "Sky's the limit. Are you ready?"

"Yes, are you?"

The nonchalant shrug couldn't mask the pain in his lovely green eyes. She turned and laid her hand against his cheek. Awareness sizzled between them. His eyes darkened, pupils dilated, and Rebecca instinctively knew he wanted to kiss her. The thought sent shivers of delight down her spine. She couldn't move and she couldn't tear her attention from his hypnotic gaze. As of their own accord, her lips lifted to receive his kiss.

Ray hesitated a moment before lowering his mouth to hers. His kiss was tentative, searching. By the tender, yet anxious way he held her—as though he expected her to bolt— their first kiss must have weighed on his mind.

She took his other hand, placed it on her waist, and then trailed her palm up his arm to cup his face gently. A little murmur of encouragement escaped her as his arms slid around her and pulled her closer. He held her lightly and deepened the kiss briefly before ending it by slow degrees.

"Hold me, Becca," he whispered, kissing first one palm then the other.

Her heart trembled as she leaned closer and slipped her arms around his neck. His lips traveled over her cheek to her ear then paused for an intimate caress of mouth against flesh.

At her soft sigh of pleasure, his lips journeyed down her throat to the pulse beating erratically at its base. He nuzzled there and then moved on to caress the slim column, to bury his face in her hair. Absently, she wondered if he noticed how deeply he affected her.

Shocked at her response, Rebecca's hands kneaded his back and shoulders in a restless gesture. She could feel the wild thump of his heart matching rhythm with her own racing pulse. As if doused with cold water, the realization of their actions slammed into her mind. Rebecca deliberately calmed the instinct to run. She didn't want to offend Ray again, not now when he was grieving, not again when she was sure it would rupture their budding relationship. She lingered in his embrace a moment then stepped away.

His arms slowly slid from around her until his hands rested on her waist. She smoothed over the tense muscles in his shoulders, down his arms and then raised his hands to her lips, kissing the back of each.

Tugging free of her grip, Ray cupped her face. A wealth of emotions clouded her mind—excitement, wonder, guilt. She lifted her gaze and peered into his eyes.

His gaze dropped to her lips, lingered there. "You have a lovely mouth."

Heat scorched her cheeks. "So do you. We need to go."

Ray pressed his lips to her forehead then took her arm and escorted her to the car without another word.

Chapter Eleven

The memorial service was quick, smooth, and uneventful. Both his parents had wanted to be cremated, so there was no funeral. As usual, his parents had even seen to that detail of their perfectly orchestrated lives.

No one ever bothered to ask Ray what he would have preferred. Which was fine since he probably wouldn't have felt the need for graveside visits with the people who'd given him life and then abandoned him to live it alone.

Though he introduced her to very few, Rebecca stood at his side accepting words of condolence and sympathy from the throng of individuals who readily accepted her offer of refreshments at his parents' home.

Gracious and attentive, she served and fetched and cleaned up behind them, making sure no food was left where it had spilled, or rings formed on the furniture from glasses left carelessly unattended or abandoned once drained of punch.

She hurried to their beck and call. Bringing more food, drink, or napkins. And listened to the endless, insincere murmurings of "how tragic" followed by "how pretty" while they fingered his mother's prized collection of crystal figurines or looked at his father's paintings.

By the time the last guest had come and gone, Ray's stomach was in knots. He wanted nothing more than to smash every last figurine and rip the paintings from their expensive frames. He turned to Rebecca, his fists clenched in an effort to control his raging emotions. "I'm going to run over to the Y and take a swim. Want to come?"

Rebecca looked around at the mess left behind and shook her head. "No. I think I'll clean up this mess and then call Jeff."

Ray picked up the phone and held it toward her. "Call a maid service. I did not bring you here to work like a dog."

Fury leapt to life in her eyes, her chin lifted in defiance. Rebecca drew herself to her full five-feet-two inches. "Don't dare talk to me in that tone of voice, Raymond Scott Jacobey. My husband never used that tone with me, neither have my children, and I will not tolerate it out of you." Her voice softened. "I'm not the enemy here, Ray."

Ray swallowed convulsively, equally stunned by his behavior. "Becca, I..."

She closed the distance between them, stopping his apology with a finger on his lips. "Go take your swim."

The compassion and understanding in her eyes only made him feel like more of a jerk. He nodded curtly, stalked up the stairs to change, grabbed an old pair of swimming trunks then stormed out of the house into the garage.

On the way to the Y, his emotions got the better of him and tears poured as he contemplated the loss of his parents, their never-ending distance towards him, and his mixed up feelings of abandonment. And then there was Becca... *Would he get the chance to change his life to a warm, loving family of his own?*

What was he doing, leaving her to clean *his* parents' house all by herself? She wasn't a maid service. She'd been attentive and kind all day—to him and to all the people who milled through the rooms as if they were attending a Sunday buffet.

On second thought, he turned the car around and headed back to the house. He didn't need a swim, he needed Becca.

When he walked in the door a few minutes later, Rebecca was sitting in a chair with her head in her hands. She lifted a startled gaze towards him.

He gave her a sheepish, one-sided smile and shrugged. "I don't want to go to the Y, Becca. I want to be with you." He glanced at the mess around them.

"Let's get started."

She shook her head and stood, came to stand right in front of him. She gazed up into his face and his heart did a girlish flutter. "I get it, Ray. I understand how lonely you must have been growing up in this big, sprawling house with your parents gone all the time. I'd hoped the memorial service would bring closure, help you to put that painful past behind you through the support of other mourners. But you were right. Those people who gathered here today weren't friends offering love or even support to the only child of colleagues killed in a tragic accident. They were snobs. Vultures seeking to see what would be up for grabs should you decide to get rid of your parents' expensive trinkets and artwork."

She lifted her hand to his face, moving her soft skin against his five o'clock shadow. The gesture, her words, the compassion in her gaze almost broke him.

"I saw it all, Ray. They ate your food, drank your beverages, and browsed as though window-shopping in an expensive boutique. No one offered true sympathy or honest compassion, much less a handshake or shoulder to cry on. And no one offered a helping hand."

He covered her hand with his and leaned into her palm.

"You did, Becca. You offered all those things, and I didn't even have to ask."

Her consideration was a balm over his hurting heart. How had he lived without her in his life for so long? How could he want her so badly, so quickly? He drew her to him, stroked a stray hair from her forehead. "You, Becca, are one special lady. Beautiful."

She glanced down at the sweats and baggy shirt she'd changed into while he was gone.

"Yes, Becca, beautiful. No matter what you're wearing." He kissed her forehead. "I know I said we'd take things slow—and we will. As slow as you like, but Becca?" He kissed her left cheek.

She closed her eyes, and he kissed each eyelid.

"Yes?"

Her quiet hum of pleasure sent little shivers of delight up his spine. "I sure hope fast is the new slow."

He kissed her smiling lips, then against all instinct, retreated a little. "I think we need to clean up this mess. What do you say?"

She nodded, slipped out of his arms, and began to clean and straighten up.

The food had been picked over so thoroughly that what little was left was disgusting. Together, they dumped it all in the trash.

The punch bowl was empty and two of the tiny, delicate cups broken. He cleaned up the shards while she carefully washed the bowl and left it on the counter to dry. Stacking cups, saucers, plates, and silverware into the dishwasher she turned it on and then focused her attention on cleaning the floor.

While he filled and tied bags of garbage, he watched her straighten the mess with silent efficiency. She walked through the rooms tugging on tablecloths and straightening knick-knacks and then dusting the mahogany furniture that his parents had acquired from all over the world. Prize possessions—unlike their son. He shook off the hurt, intent on focusing on Rebecca. As he carried the trash outside, his mind formed plans for the evening. As he passed his mother's prize rosebush, he snapped a few stems and arranged the roses into a makeshift bouquet.

When he reentered the kitchen, Rebecca met him at the door. "Thanks for helping me. I wouldn't have minded you going for a swim, you know."

This was his Becca, sweet, innocent, lovely. "You went above and beyond with the arrangements, the food—the cleaning." Ray held the roses out to her.

She took the flowers and buried her nose in the pale, pink petals. "It's no trouble. It's what I do best. Remember? Are you hungry?" she asked, turning toward the kitchen.

"A little," he admitted, following in her wake.

"Well, there wasn't much left but crumbs considering all the food I prepared this morning, but I can whip up something."

Ray shook his head. "No, you can't. I'm taking you out to dinner."

Becca looked down at her sweats and baggy shirt with a frown. "But that means I'll have to change—and shower."

Ray laughed. "We'll order in then. But you still have to shower." He grinned and leaned in to place a quick kiss on her cheek.

She playfully smacked his arm.

He moved to the counter where the phone lay. "Pizza or Chinese?"

"Mmm. Chinese." She filled a vase with water, placed the roses in it and set the vase on the table. Then she headed upstairs.

Moments later, he heard the water running.

Ray called in the food order then set the table, opting for the small one in the breakfast nook as opposed to the huge conglomerate in the formal dining room. He flanked the vase of roses with crystal candelabras that his mother had bought in France. The pale green candles complemented the soft pink rose petals. Then he found his mother's prized English china—the set hand-painted with a delicate rose pattern. Resisting the urge to release some emotional frustration at his parents, he set down dinner plates instead of smashing the dishes on the floor. A pitcher of ice water garnished with lemon slices and strawberries completed the task.

By the time he'd created the romantic setting he wanted to present, the water from the bathroom had stopped running so he went upstairs to take his own shower.

Rebecca sat at the dressing table and brushed her hair. Her mind whirled at Ray's sweetness and the way he'd pitched in to help her clean after the guests traipsed through the house. Her heart still ached for the childhood he'd missed. Thinking of which, she took a moment to call Jeff, but got his voicemail instead. She left a message that she was fine, and she'd try to reach him at a later time. At the sound of water running in the adjacent bath, she went downstairs to wait for Ray. She answered the door when the food arrived and hesitated in the doorway of the spacious kitchen. The set table, roses, and candles whispered romance and made her heart flutter. She sensed more than heard him walk up behind her only moments before his arms encircled her waist.

She smiled. "You set a lovely table, Ray."

He grinned and then skimmed his lips over her cheek.

"Who says takeout has to be simple or plain?"

He placed his hand at her elbow, led her to the table and pulled out a chair for her to sit, then took his own across from her. While she served the food, he lit candles and poured water into the goblets beside their plates.

Rebecca couldn't recall a time she'd enjoyed dinner more, except for maybe their first date at his house back home

Chapter Twelve

The next day proved to be every bit as difficult as the one before. Ray's meeting with his parents' attorney to go over stipulations of the will was set for ten o'clock. At Ray's request, Rebecca accompanied him.

She sat, shocked into silence at the exorbitant sums that made up the value of properties and artwork the Jacobey's owned. She watched with concern as Ray paced the small space across the width of the office, tension oozing from every pore of his being.

"Do you want to do this another time, Raymond?" the attorney asked.

"I don't want to do it at all." He snorted. "Just give me the bottom line."

Rebecca's mind reeled at the amount the lawyer rattled off. Though her husband had left her well provided for, never had she imagined such wealth.

Ray seemed equally stunned. His eyes narrowed. His jaw clenched as tightly as the fists by his side. "Let me ask you something." He addressed the attorney in a voice taut with disgust. "Are there any special requests for gifts to friends or donations to favorite charities?"

The attorney shook his head. "No. It all goes to you. What do you want to do with it?"

He shrugged. "Sell it, give it away, burn it to the ground."

"Your parents worked hard all of their lives to get where they are and to provide for you, Raymond. I'd hate to see it all go to waste because of some unreasonable sense of pride you may have."

Ray turned on the attorney in an angry whirl. "Unreasonable, my ass. My parents worked hard all of their lives to provide for themselves. They were selfish and self-centered. Fancy cars, fancy schools, fancy toys, everything they ever gave me only increased their own prestige. I was raised by nannies and babysitters. I was never invited to come home for holidays after I left. I was obviously unwanted. I interfered in their goals for themselves, and when they were done being forced to take care of me, I got a generous birthday card and an even more generous Christmas card once a year. That was it. Their wealth meant nothing to me then. It means even less to me now so you can take your opinion of me and shove it where the sun don't shine."

Rebecca gasped, simultaneously shocked at the suppressed anger and empathetic of the hurt Ray still carried from the neglect of his parents. She rose from her chair. "Stop it Ray."

Her soft, firm voice had all eyes focused on her. Apparently surprised by the thread of steel in her tone, Ray visibly swallowed the remainder of his wrath.

Rebecca readdressed the attorney. "Does he have to make any major decisions today? Surely there's enough in available cash to leave things as they are for a while."

"Of course, there is."

"OK." She took a deep breath and tried to think. "What about the bills, utilities and such?"

"I'll have them discontinued."

Rebecca thought of the food in the freezer and refrigerator. "No, don't do that. Just make sure they get paid and leave everything else as it is until he's ready to deal with it."

The attorney nodded. "Is that acceptable to you, Raymond?"

"Whatever," Ray muttered, turning on his heel and stalking out of the office.

"I'm sorry. He needs time to work through it all," Rebecca whispered, blinking back tears on Ray's behalf. Suddenly she knew that both she and Ray had a lot of healing to do before either of them could consider a future together.

"Don't worry about it. I've heard it all before," the attorney said, his voice kind. Rising from his chair, he escorted her to the door.

She found Raymond waiting in the car.

Total, strained silence accompanied them the entire ride back to the house. Rebecca put her hand on his in a gesture of support, felt him stiffen, and wondered if she'd overstepped her boundaries.

Ray roared into the garage and slammed out of the car, leaving her to get out on her own.

Rebecca hurried after him. His hand trembled and he fumbled to unlock the door, so she took the keys and opened it herself.

Once inside he crumbled. "I never wanted their money, Becca. I only wanted their love and support, or at least their approval. Here I am a grown man, still wanting Mommy and Daddy to love me, still wishing things were different. I tried to keep in touch with them, to call them on their birthdays and at Christmas, but they rebuffed me. I was never asked back into their lives after I left home, yet they left everything to me. Why?"

Taking him gently by the arm, Rebecca led Ray to the couch as he began to weep, huge, heaving sobs that shook his entire frame and tore at her heart.

"I don't ever recall hearing them say they loved me. I can't remember ever saying it to them."

Tears streamed down her cheeks. Rebecca climbed onto his lap and encircled her arms around him. Her hands moved over his back and shoulders in a soothing caress.

"I want to go home, now. How long will it take you to get ready?" he asked, his voice wrought with emotion.

"Ten minutes."

"Let's go."

They were ready in less than ten minutes.

Rebecca took the keys from Ray and drove to the airport. She turned in the rental car and redeemed their tickets. They managed to catch a flight out in less than an hour. They made the flight home in silence, though it was much less tense than before. Rebecca held Ray's hand the entire time, offering her support in quiet assurance. Only when the plane touched down at SeaTac Airport did he begin to relax.

An hour later, Rebecca unlocked the door to her house and sighed with relief. Ray stepped in behind her and set down her luggage.

"How about a sandwich and a cup of coffee or tea?"

Ray raised her fingers to his lips, kissed the tips. "No thanks, I'll get something at home. Thanks for everything Becca, I..." He cleared his throat and swallowed hard. "I appreciate all you've done and I'm grateful to have you in my life."

Rebecca touched his cheek with a tender smile, sensing he wanted to say more. "As I do you, Ray. Be careful and please call me when you get home, so I'll know you made it safe."

"I will." He backed out of the door and waited until she closed and locked it before leaving.

While waiting for him to call, Rebecca unpacked her suitcase, checked, and watered her plants, fixed herself a cup of herbal tea and thought about all that had happened in two short days. If there was a lesson in all this, it was never to let an opportunity pass to show appreciation for the ones you love. Knowing she wouldn't reach either of her children at home, she called anyway, leaving messages on their answering machines that she was home and safe and how very much she loved them.

Ray dragged his suitcase out of the car and carried it into his apartment. Numb with exhaustion, he dropped it on the living room floor, vowing to unpack later. He called Rebecca as promised, told her he was home and safe, agreed to try to get some rest and assured her that he'd call her again soon.

He considered phoning work and going in tomorrow but decided against it. He'd taken a week off to go to Flagstaff and had used only two days. He'd go back as scheduled if he went back at all.

If he accepted his parents' money, he never had to work another day in his life. The realization hit him hard. He was rich, now yielded a fortune that rivaled that of some of the wealthiest people in America.

He'd only had to become an orphan to get it.

The loneliness that had been so much a part of him

intensified at the thought, and Ray realized he'd lost more than his parents in that accident. He'd lost hope. For as long as he could remember, he'd dreamed that one day his parents would grow to love—or at least come to appreciate—him for the boy he'd been or the man he'd become. Now, all hope of that dream coming true was lost. He felt desolate, barren, like a desert in desperate need of rain.

Stripping as he went, Ray headed for the bathroom and stood a long time under the pulsating spray, hoping the hot shower would sear the pain from his heart and mind. When it failed, and the water ran tepid, he slapped the faucet off, rubbed a towel over his body, draped it around his waist and then stretched out on his bed.

He lay there broken and empty and overwhelmed with grief. Tears rolled unchecked down his cheeks until, spent, he fell into an exhausted slumber, one arm over his eyes. The other stretched out beside him as though reaching for someone. Someone to hold. Someone to love.

Chapter Thirteen

Ray awoke sometime after midnight, groggy, disoriented and so hungry he'd have sworn his stomach had gnawed a hole in his backbone. Getting up, he traded the towel for a robe, and made a sandwich. It tasted like cardboard and felt like sawdust going down but filled the empty spot in his belly.

Numb except for the aching hole in his heart, he wandered into the living room. He picked up the suitcase from where he'd dropped it earlier, unpacked, and then sat on the edge of his bed. He buried his face in trembling hands as he thought about his life.

All the years of prayer and meditation, of faith and trust in the power of God's love and grace, disappeared when he considered his behavior these past two days. He realized the healing he'd sought was far from complete. Not only incomplete, but also hindered by bitterness and unforgiveness—emotions that had lain dormant in his heart until two days ago.

Rebecca will probably never speak to me again.

This time the tears he shed weren't of grief or loneliness, but of sorrow and repentance. Purged of every emotion, save pain, he cried out to God for understanding, and was rewarded when He answered. *"Though a nursing mother forgets her child, yet I will never leave you nor forsake you."*

In that instant, Ray knew that no matter how his parents felt about him, God had always been there, giving him the strength to go on and to keep hoping. But it was up to him to let go once and for all, let go and let God do the healing he'd failed so miserably to accomplish.

Understanding followed enlightenment. Oh, he'd prayed and believed and worked hard at forgiving his parents. So hard, in fact, that he actually believed he had, and was proud of himself for doing so. That pride had been his downfall. He may have convinced his mind he'd forgiven them, but only God could change a heart.

Stretching out on the bed once more, he began to pray for God to take away the pain, bitterness and unforgiveness in his heart, and to bring to light the good in his parents.

Rebecca bit back her disappointment and smiled at the letter carrier when he handed her the mail. On the porch table sat a tray loaded with fresh sandwiches and homemade soup. She hadn't heard from Ray since he dropped her off the day before yesterday. Figuring he needed some time to himself, she respected his privacy expecting that today he would be back on the job, and they would talk over lunch. Concerned now, she carried the tray back inside and thought about calling him.

Instead, she heated up the soup and poured it into a large, wide-mouth thermos. She covered the sandwiches in cellophane, loaded everything into a picnic basket and headed over to his apartment. She'd parked the car, grabbed the basket and was two steps away from knocking, when the door opened, and a young woman stepped out. Ray walked out behind her.

Stunned, Rebecca hesitated in her tracks.

"Thanks, Jan," he said to the young woman.

"No problem. Anytime. Take care, and if you need anything, don't hesitate to call."

"Will do. Oh, Becca, hi!" His entire countenance lit up when he noticed her for the first time since walking out of the apartment.

A flush rushed to Rebecca's cheeks. "Hi. I didn't realize you had company. Guess I should have called first."

A smile lit his eyes, tugged at his lips. "Nonsense, you don't ever have to call first."

He pointed to the young woman. "Becca, this is Jan. Jan, Rebecca Sinclair."

Rebecca smiled and nodded.

Jan returned the greeting then glanced back at Ray. "See ya later, Ray." She gave a little wave, before walking away.

Rebecca watched until Jan got into her car and left then faced Ray once more, arching an eyebrow.

He reached for the picnic basket. "What'cha got there?"

She held it out of his reach. "I made us some lunch. When you didn't show, I thought I'd come and check on you. Seems there was no need."

As if he sensed her unease, Ray gave her a reassuring smile. "Jan is a friend from work. She lives just up the road a ways, so she dropped off my check and some other paperwork for me. I invited her in for a cup of coffee, Becca, nothing more." He cupped her cheeks in his hands. "There's only room in my heart for one woman, Becca, and that woman is you." He captured her lips in a tender kiss.

Rebecca's heart did a slow swirl into her stomach. "Glad to hear it. Are you hungry?"

"For your cooking, always." He took the basket from her while slipping one arm around her waist and escorted her into his apartment. "Here or the patio?" he asked when they reached the kitchen.

Rebecca couldn't suppress the sharp pang of jealousy at the sight of the empty coffee cups. She had no right to be jealous. "In here is fine," she said, determined not to act like a fool.

Ray set down the basket and chuckled.

"Something funny, Ray?"

He removed the coffee cups from the table and put them in the sink. "Not a thing," he said, reaching for her.

"Then wipe that silly grin off your face."

Ray tossed back his head with a laugh. "Yes, Ma'am." He swooped her up and twirled her. "Boy, I missed talking to you yesterday." He settled her back on her feet.

Rebecca laid her hand against his cheek. "I missed you, too. But I figured you needed some time to yourself."

He covered her hand with his, moved it to his lips, kissed the palm and pulled her a notch closer.

Rebecca placed a firm hand on his chest. "Let's eat while it's still hot."

"One kiss."

"N—"

His lips took sweet possession of hers. "Thank you," he whispered against her mouth.

Surprised at the sweet lethargy that infused her bones as he released her from his grasp, Rebecca reached for the back of a chair.

"What would you like to drink?"

"Tea." Figuring she'd just have to get used to the way her body responded every time he took her in his arms, she collapsed into the chair.

Ray poured their drinks while Rebecca unloaded the picnic basket.

Over soup and sandwiches, he told her of the revelation he'd had regarding his parents and the forgiveness he thought he'd accomplished. "I've been such a fool, Becca."

"You're not a fool, Ray. You're human. The world has insulated us against love, taught us that compassion is useless, and that forgiveness shows weakness. Therefore, it's not as easy as it should be."

"I have to go back."

"You need to find some peace, and you need to make peace with your past and your parents. Even if it's only in your own heart."

"I know, and I think the only way I'll be able to do that is to go back. Besides, I have to figure out what to do with that monstrosity of a house."

Rebecca smiled at his choice of words but refrained from comment.

"I took an extended leave of absence, Becca. That's the paperwork Jan brought by."

A flicker of annoyance licked her insides at the mention of the other woman's name, but it didn't affect her nearly as much as the thought of not seeing Ray every day. "How long will you be gone?" she asked, hoping the ache in her heart didn't reflect in her voice or eyes.

Ray shrugged. "A week or two, I guess. Depends on how long it takes to go through the house and figure out what to keep, what to get rid of and how to get rid of it." As if on impulse, he grabbed her hand. "Come with me."

Though it shouldn't have, his request surprised her. "What?"

"Come with me. It'll be like a vacation. I promise we'll do some sightseeing this time."

"But I can't stay gone for an indefinite period of time. I have plants to water and kids to think of."

"OK, we'll only stay a week or so, two at most. The plants will be fine. The kids aren't coming home until Christmas, and it's not even Halloween yet. You can call them every day if you want, Becca. Whatever it takes. Just come with me."

"When are you leaving?"

"Today, tomorrow, as soon as we can get packed. Thought I'd drive down this time. It'll only take a couple of days."

She hesitated.

"You trust me, don't you, Becca? You're not afraid to be with me like that are you?"

"Of course, I trust you. I'm not afraid at all. I'm just wondering what my kids will say about me gallivanting all over creation with you."

He chuckled. "I'm sure you'll be able to alleviate any misgivings they might have. We'll have to stay overnight in hotels, so we'll get separate rooms."

"It's time you start thinking and feeling for yourself."

The counselor's words floated through her mind.

Rebecca agreed. It was time for her to start thinking about what she wanted, what would make her happy. And to stop worrying about what everyone else might think.

Vacations with her family had always been a stressful time. The kids argued and fussed or sulked because they didn't want to go to begin with.

Jim was his usual orderly self, insisting that everything be kept in its place, and they always went somewhere educational—a war memorial or some military museum. There was never really much time for relaxing. Not for Rebecca anyway.

Going with Ray to Flagstaff would be fun. And what better way for them to get to know one another? She squeezed his hand. "OK, Ray. I'll go with you."

"Great! Let's leave today, right now. Go home, pack a suitcase or two, call your kids—leave a message if you have to—and I'll pick you up in an hour."

Feeling like a little girl going off on a grand adventure, Rebecca allowed those giddy emotions to push away the doubts and concerns. She packed a suitcase and an overnight bag, put the plants which needed the most care out on the porch where they could catch water if it rained, and prayed the temperature didn't drop too low within the next couple of weeks. She decided not to call her kids until she and Ray stopped for the night.

Ray knocked on her door and entered at her invitation. "Ready yet?"

Rebecca nodded.

"Good. I had our mail put on vacation hold."

She hadn't thought about that. Her eyes widened. A flush warmed her cheeks. "You should have let me do that so everyone wouldn't know I'm going with you."

He squeezed her hand. "The only person who knows is Jan, and she promised to be very discreet about putting in the requests."

Annoyance sparked inside her. She crossed her arms over her chest. "How well do you know this woman?"

Ray chuckled. "Jealousy is usually a very ugly emotion, but on you it's adorable."

He reached for her, but she stepped out of his grasp. "Don't mock me, Ray."

He took a step forward, closed the distance she'd put between them and cupped her cheeks in his hands. "I'd never mock you."

"And don't kiss me." She poked a finger in his chest to stop him from doing just that.

She shook her head, and he released her. "I'm not that easy to distract, and I am not jealous. Well, maybe a little jealous." She huffed at his arched brow. "But that's not the point. The point is that you know I've been married over half my life to the same man, a man that—as far as I know—was faithful to me. I know nothing about your personal life. I'm not used to being around a man who's been single all his life and may have slept with hundreds of women. I want to know how well you know this one."

Ray stepped away from her, smiled. "I know her about as well as I'd know any good friend or maybe a close cousin. We dated. Once. Dinner and a movie, I think. When I kissed her goodnight, it was so dispassionate we both ended up laughing. We've been friends ever since."

Ray cupped her face in his hands again. "And, Becca," his voice lowered a notch, "I've not had any meaningful relationships."

She let out a breath and placed her hand on his cheek. "Thank you."

"You're welcome. Now may I kiss you?" Without waiting for permission, his lips captured hers in a scorching embrace. He hugged her firmly. His mouth clung to hers, molding and shaping it until each ragged breath she took became one with his.

He ended the kiss by slow degrees.

"Don't kiss me like that again, Ray." She ran a trembling hand through her hair.

"Why not?"

He looked as though he might pull her back in his arms and do it again, so she stepped away. The passion that sparked between them rivaled anything she'd experienced. She had to be mindful of that. "Because I can't handle it when you do. I'm not ready to handle it yet. Promise, or I won't go with you."

"That will be a difficult promise to keep, but I'll try."

"Then maybe I shouldn't go."

His expression saddened. "I thought you trusted me."

A twinge of guilt pricked her as she looked into his troubled gaze. "I do trust you. But…I'm not used to being kissed like that by anyone but my husband. I don't believe in premarital sex, Ray, and I don't want to spend the entire trip fighting you off."

His pained expression brightened into a beaming smile. "Then marry me. We'll take a quick detour through Vegas and get hitched in one of those little twenty-four hour wedding chapels."

His grin was charming, boyish. His eyes danced with humor. Though she knew he was probably teasing, Rebecca heard the underlying thread of sincerity in his proposal. Panic bubbled up to choke her. "I can't marry you. We've only known each other—"

"A year. People get married all the time to someone they've dated less time than that."

"We've known each other a year, dated less than a month," she corrected.

He clasped her hand and raised it to his lips. "OK, Becca, I promise not to kiss you like that again. Unless you initiate it of course," he added with a teasing grin, and then sobered. "I promise not to compromise you or your values, especially since mine are the same. You won't have to fight me off," he assured, in a tone devoid of laughter.

Rebecca hesitated a moment, searching his eyes for assurance of the promise he'd just made. "OK Ray, I believe you. But you'd better believe me when I say I'll break your hands if you get too forward."

Ray tossed his head back and laughed. He let go of her hand and picked up her suitcase. "I believe you," he said, but his eyes were alive with wicked humor.

Chapter Fourteen

"What's this?" Ray asked when Rebecca handed him some papers before climbing into the front seat of his SUV.

"I went online and printed out a map and directions for our trip."

He chuckled. "That's what GPS is for."

She flushed. "Oh, I didn't think of that. Besides, wouldn't this be much easier than trying to read directions on that tiny screen?"

"Probably so, but it is voice activated, too."

She shook her head, laughed. "Men and their toys."

"Hey, women use technology."

"Not me. I'd rather have written directions." She took the papers back from him and studied the printout. The directions took them clear across Washington before turning south through Idaho, Utah, and then on to Arizona. "Maybe we should use your GPS. This looks like the long way there."

Ray pulled up the app on his phone, keyed in the info and compared the readout to what Rebecca had printed. "Looks about the same to me. I think it's supposed to be the quickest route."

Rebecca shook her head. "The shortest distance between two points is a straight line," she insisted, remembering the many times she'd had to remind her kids of that during their years of high-school math. The memory made her smile.

"What's the smile for?"

Blood singed her cheeks. "Oh, just remembering helping

my kids with their math homework. Jeffrey hated it, said he only needed to know how to count to eight. On the other hand, Debbie loved it. That and science."

"They're blessed to have you for a mom."

Rebecca heard the longing in his voice. She reached over and stroked his cheek with the back of her hand. "Your parents were blessed to have you."

"I'm praying to remember the good, Becca. But it's hard. I never realized how truly bitter I was until it dawned on me I couldn't remember anything good. I don't ever remember sharing the kind of love with them that you share with your kids. I don't even know if they did love me or want me, or if I just came along and they didn't know what else to do but keep me."

Not wanting to dredge up more bad memories and start their trip on a sour note, Rebecca spoke what was in her heart, but chose her words with care. "Most parents love their children, Ray. Maybe they just didn't know how to show it. You've said they were very busy, high-strung people. Maybe they figured all it took to be good parents was to provide well for you. The things you disparage so much—the fancy schools, fancy toys, fancy clothes, the nannies, the money—maybe that was their way of showing you how much they cared."

She placed a hand on his arm. "Many parents struggle to provide even the barest necessities for their children, and most people only dream of the kind of wealth your parents have left you. They've made it so you don't have to work another day in your life and can still leave an inheritance for your children's children. If that idea doesn't appeal to you, think of the good you can do with it, the people you can help, and the lives you can bless. I know it's a sore spot for you, Ray, and I don't want to sound as if I'm getting on my soap box here, but maybe you should try to think about it without so much emotion."

Ray nodded. "I've been praying to do just that, but I don't want to think about it too much right now. Let's just enjoy the trip down. There's enough time to be serious when we get there."

Rebecca agreed and prayed silently that she could help him remember the good in his parents. "OK, speaking of which, there's got to be a quicker way to Flagstaff."

Ray shook his head as he stopped at a red light. "No matter which way we go, we have to go through Vegas. I figure I've got a day-and-a-half to get you into one of those twenty-four-hour wedding chapels."

His eyes danced with mirth.

Rebecca bit back a smile. "Don't you dare start with that, Ray. I'll make you turn this car around and take me home."

Ray laughed and eased off the brake as the light changed and traffic began to move.

The hours seemed to fly by as quickly as the miles. Some of the conversations they shared were of a serious nature. Most were not. They talked and joked and laughed until tears of hilarity streamed down their cheeks.

They spent the night at a Bed & Breakfast in Spokane, Washington where Ray bought her flowers fresh from nearby luxurious gardens.

The next day they drove through Idaho and Utah, taking time out to enjoy a train tour of Boise and a walking tour of historic Salt Lake City, then spent the night at a cozy little inn just outside Utah's capitol.

By the time they arrived in Flagstaff both were exhausted.

Ray pulled into the garage of his family home with a sigh of relief. "I never thought I'd be happy to see this place."

Rebecca hummed in agreement. "A hot shower or bath, home-cooked meal and nice, soft bed, see there is some good."

He chuckled as he got out of the car and unlocked the door to the house.

Rebecca followed, content but weary from the hours spent couped up in the vehicle.

"You don't have to cook, you know? I'll order something to be delivered."

"After three days on the road I'm tired of everyone else's cooking," Rebecca said.

"So am I. But we're both exhausted, and I don't want you to go to a lot of trouble."

Rebecca cupped his cheek in her hand. "It's no trouble. I'll make us something light and fresh and delicious. You take a shower and relax."

Ray covered her hand with his, moved it to his lips, kissed her palm, then left a tiny trail of kisses to her wrist while he slid his arm around her waist and pulled her against him.

"Ray." She put a restraining hand on his chest.

"Becca," he murmured, as his lips began a sensuous journey across her forehead, lingered briefly at her temple, and then left a trail of moist fire across her cheek to her lips. "One little kiss." He nibbled at the corners of her mouth while pulling her tighter against his chest. "Then I just want to hold you."

She strained against the hold he had on her despite her weakened knees and desire to remain in his arms. "There's nothing little about your kisses."

He grinned against her mouth, continued to nibble at her lips. "Really? Good, 'cause I want you thinking only of me when I kiss you." He captured her mouth in a brief, gentle kiss.

Rebecca forced herself to remain tense in his arms when all instinct had her melting like ice exposed to sunlight. "You promised, Ray...."

He continued to nip and taste the sensitive skin around her mouth, keeping the kisses light, teasing. "I promised I wouldn't compromise you or your values, Becca, and I'm not. I won't." He maintained a steady assault to her senses. "I haven't kissed you, really kissed you in more than two days. I want to now. Hold me, trust me."

Surrendering to his plea and her pleasure, she clasped her arms around his neck, relaxed against him, and returned the embrace.

Ray's hands plunged into the thick, silky mass of her hair while his mouth plundered hers. Within moments, she was grappling for self-control.

Suddenly, he jerked his mouth away from hers and buried his face in her neck. "Sweet heavens, that was more intense than I bargained for. More than I intended."

Her pulse beat erratically against his lips, her body quivered, her cheeks were wet with tears she hadn't realized she'd shed.

"Are you all right?"

Rebecca clung to him, stripped of every ounce of strength, devoid of even the slightest hint of reason. "Hold me Ray. If you turn me loose now you'll have to scrape me up off the floor," she mumbled, as sobs began to shake her slender frame.

"Geeze, don't cry, Rebecca. Please don't cry."

"I've never felt like this before." Unanticipated anger pushed past the raw emotions thrumming through her body. "Do you know how it makes me feel to say that, to admit that my husband—the man I loved for twenty-two years—didn't move me with a single kiss the way you do?"

For long moments, Ray remained silent. Then he pressed her face against his chest, stroked her hair in a soothing gesture. "I can imagine, Becca."

The tenderness in his voice made her cry harder. "It makes me feel disloyal and disrespectful of him, his memory and of the love we shared."

"I would never ask you to forget the love you shared with your husband or to compare it with what you feel for me, what we feel for each other." He raked in a deep breath. "I love you, Becca."

His admission undid her even more. "I—I know-you d-do. And what makes it even worse is that I'm not entirely sure of my feelings yet. I do care about you, a great deal, and I don't ever want to hurt you."

He cuddled her gently and continued to stroke her hair. "It's OK, Becca. I've waited all my life for a woman like you. I can wait a while longer."

Her trembling stopped. Her sobs subsided into soft, hiccupping sounds as she won the battle to get her emotions under control.

Ray released her from his embrace and cupped her face in his hands. "But know this," he whispered. "I'll never give up and I'll never let you go. I've waited too long to say those words to chicken out now. But I won't kiss you like that again. Not until you're ready, not until you're sure."

Rebecca studied his face. For in that instant, she knew she loved him too, had since the very first time their lips met, possibly before. Still, she withheld her declaration, vowing that when she said the words, he'd have no reason to doubt her sincerity. She rubbed her knuckles over his cheek. "Thank you, Ray. Now, go take your shower while I fix us a bite to eat."

"Yes, Ma'am."

Rebecca rummaged around in the freezer and spotted a package of boneless, skinless chicken breasts. She took it out and defrosted it in the microwave. Frozen vegetables and a bag of brown rice gave her the ingredients for a quick stir-fry supper. She added a can of fruit cocktail, and they had a full course meal.

Ray insisted on cleaning the kitchen so she could relax in a hot shower or bath.

Though she longed to soak in a hot tub of frothy water, Rebecca chose a shower instead so she could wash her hair. She stood a long time under the pulsating spray and thought about her feelings for Ray. That she loved him came as no real surprise. He was the kind of man any woman could love–sweet, gentle, kind. He had the sense of humor of an innocent child and an inner strength that subtly assured others he was more than capable of holding his own if pushed into a confrontation.

Rebecca had no doubt she would be loved, protected, and well cared for should they ever marry. And therein lay the problem. A man like Raymond would want marriage and children, and though she wasn't totally against the idea of being married again or even having more children, she wasn't sure she wanted it so soon or at all. She'd raised her children and looked forward to grandchildren. Besides, another baby at her age could be dangerous. Rebecca shook her head to quell the thoughts. *Getting way too ahead of yourself. This is all something to talk over and work out later.*

Finishing her shower, Rebecca dressed in a t-shirt and sweats and combed out her hair. Opting to let it dry by itself, she decided to call Jeffrey. Though she'd called nightly, she hadn't actually talked to him and was thrilled when he answered.

"Hey, Mom, how's it going?"

"Fine, have you gotten my messages?"

"Yeah, and I know you're gallivanting all over God's creation with that guy. Is everything OK? You sound down."

The disgruntled tone of her son's voice made her smile. "Everything's fine. I'm just tired, sweetheart."

"So, where are you now and how long will you be there?"

"We arrived in Flagstaff, at his parents' house a little while ago. I imagine we'll stay here about a week or so and then head back home."

"Are you sure this is a good idea? Do you really know and trust this guy? I know you said you think he's in love with you but—"

"Yes, I really trust him. And I was right. He is very much in love with me."

"How do you feel about him?"

Rebecca cringed at the edge in her son's voice. "I care about him a great deal, Jeff. But it's all mixed up with grief and loneliness and confusion right now."

"Confusion, what kind of confusion? He hasn't tried anything with you, has he? I'll kill him if he has!"

Rebecca smiled at the receiver. "No, nothing like that, and I don't like your choice of words."

"I'm sorry Mom, but I just don't like it."

"Why not?"

"It's just not right, you and him alone like that."

"Has New York hardened you so much that you honestly believe a man and a woman can't be alone together without it being a sordid affair? Or are you judging my relationship with Ray by your own lifestyle choices?"

"N-No, Ma'am," Jeff stuttered. "Neither. Just worried I guess."

Rebecca could tell by his subdued tone that Jeff remembered the morals she'd raised him with. "Well, don't worry, honey. He's a really sweet guy. I care about him a great deal and I trust him implicitly. And I can't wait for you to meet him."

Jeff mumbled noncommittally. Rebecca giggled.

"I love you, Mom, and I don't want to see you hurt. You've been alone for over a year, and I imagine you're lonely and vulnerable right now. Just be careful and make sure this Ray guy knows he'll answer to me if he hurts you in any way."

"I'm more afraid I'll be the one to do the hurting," Rebecca admitted in a quiet voice.

"You really do care about him, don't you?"

"Yes, I care about him, a lot."

Jeff sighed. "Well, just don't do anything I wouldn't do."

Though he was teasing, Rebecca heard the underlying tension in her son's voice and instinctively knew there would be issues to face and work out with her children before she could even consider becoming a wife again. "I won't if you won't," she assured him in a soft voice. "Oh, by the way, did I tell you that young foreign man came back to the house?"

"No, when?"

"The day Ray got the call about his parents. I meant to tell you then, but with everything going on, it slipped my mind."

"What did he want?"

"Seems his mother knew your dad, or she met him one of the times he was in Korea. Anyway, she encouraged her son to look him up while he's here in the US at school."

"What's his name?"

Rebecca frowned. "You know, I didn't even think to ask. Like I said, everything happened so fast."

"You didn't let him in the house, or anything did you?"

"Of course, I let him in," Rebecca exclaimed, surprised her son would even ask such a question.

"Why, Mom? Now this guy knows you're alone! He may even be casing the place to rob it or something. Especially with you being gone for heaven-knows- how-long! I can't believe this!"

Rebecca's hair stood on end at the tone of her son's voice. "You watch your manners, young man. You may be clear across the country, but I'm not afraid to fly over there and take you to task." Rubbing her now-throbbing temples, she sighed. "I can't believe you're so paranoid, Jeffery. You need to calm down."

"I'm paranoid?" he asked, his tone incredulous. "If I'm paranoid then you're irresponsible! Letting some stranger into the house. Don't you watch the news?"

Rebecca stiffened. "No, I don't, and maybe you should

stop watching it. You're letting things you can't control consume you. I can't believe you're so narrow-minded and judgmental. You worry me. Maybe it's time for you to come home for a while and take a break. Forget New York and all the glitz, glamour and gutter you're in the midst of."

Jeff sighed then groaned. "I'm sorry, Mom. Guess I overreacted. I just worry about you all alone. There are so many psychos out there."

"I appreciate your concern for me, Jeff. But regardless of what you think, I'm not irresponsible. I lock my doors and windows. I watch out when I leave and come home. I'm careful. But I refuse to live my life in fear of my fellow man. The Bible says that he who fears man doesn't trust God. Maybe you ought to read yours more often and learn to trust again."

He apologized again.

"Apology accepted," Rebecca assured, wishing she could put her arms around her son. "Guess I'd better let you go for now, honey. I'll talk to you again in a few days and see you at Christmas. I love you."

"Love you, too, Mom."

Chapter Fifteen

Ray hesitated a moment before knocking on the half-open door of the guest room. He hadn't wanted to interrupt her conversation, nor had he intended to eavesdrop, but when he realized she was discussing her feelings for him, he wondered what she would say. He swallowed his disappointment that he hadn't heard her confess love for him.

At her soft command to enter, he stepped through the doorway. She was clad in sweats, and a t-shirt, her feet bare, face flushed, eyes sparkling. Damp hair clung to her neck and shoulders, and his hands trembled with the desire to run through that thick mass and expose her lovely neck. His grip tightened on the tray he carried lest it slip from his shaking hands. "I made us some tea," his said, his voice so thick he could barely get the words past his raw throat.

His gaze swept over her then lingered on her lips. He watched the color rise in her cheeks, and it made him want to take her in his arms. But he knew shouldn't.

She cleared her throat. "I'll be down in a minute," she said, tugging at her shirt.

He flashed a grin. "But it's hot now," he insisted with a mock pout as he set the tray on the table in the sitting area that adjoined the bedroom.

"I don't think it's very proper having tea in my bedroom."

Ray chuckled and walked to the bed where she sat. "But it's not your bedroom, Becca." He reached for her hand and pulled her to her feet. "It's mine." He wiggled his eyebrows.

Rebecca rolled her eyes. "You are incorrigible, Raymond."

He laughed and led her to the table. "And you, my darling, are beautiful." He rubbed his lips across her forehead as he pulled out the chair for her. Once she'd sat, he hauled another chair from in front of the window, sat across from her and poured them each a cup of tea. "Did I hear you talking to Jeff?"

Her eyes sparkled like rare, precious jewels when Rebecca smiled and relayed part of her conversation with Jeff to him. "He said to make sure you know that you'll answer to him if I get hurt in any way."

Ray chuckled.

"I can't wait for you to meet him. I'm afraid he'll be sulky and overprotective until he sees for himself what a terrific guy you are."

Ray lifted her hand to his lips. "I hope so, because I'm in your life to stay."

Rebecca flushed and removed her hand from his grasp.

"You sounded a bit upset there toward the end of your conversation. Is everything OK?"

A frown creased her brow. Worry darkened her eyes. "Yeah, he's a bit upset because I let a stranger in the house."

"You let a stranger in the house? Who? When?"

"It's just a kid, Ray. A young man. He came by one morning asking for Jim. At first, I thought he was a solicitor or something, so I slammed the door in his face. The next time he came by was the same evening you got the call about your parents' deaths. Before I could close the door on him, he apologized for being a bother and asked a couple of questions about Jim.

"It seems his mother met Jim on one of the occasions he

was in Korea, and she encouraged her son to look him up while going to school here in the States. When I told Jeff, he blew up." She shook her head with a sigh and took a sip of her tea. "I really worry about him sometimes. He gets so uptight about the simplest things."

Concerned green eyes searched hers for a long moment before Ray put down his cup. "Well, Jeff's got a point, Becca. With all the psychos and serial killers out there, you've got to be careful."

Rebecca rolled her eyes. "Oh, no, not you, too. Don't tell me I've got two paranoid males on my hands."

Ray laughed at her expression then sobered. "Not paranoid, we just worry about you, and rightly so. This kid, did he upset or frighten you in any way?"

"No." Rebecca scoffed. "There was nothing frightening or intimidating about him in the least. Like I said, he's just a kid. I mean, think about it. He's alone in a foreign country, hundreds of miles away from home and anything familiar. He's probably just lonely."

"Well, I trust your judgment on this, Becca. But promise you'll be careful."

"I always am and will continue to be."

"Good," Ray answered. "Now, gotta question for you. With all that's happened with my parents and the inheritance, have you thought about your letter?"

She frowned at him. "No, I haven't thought about the letter."

He eyed her. "Not even a little?" He chuckled when she flushed.

Rebecca threw her napkin at him. "Stop that."

"What?"

"Reading my mind. How come it's so easy for you to get

inside my head?"

Ray laughed. "Because your purity and sweetness make you an open book." He rose from his seat, offered his hand, and urged her to her feet. "Now, if you'll excuse me, milady, I think I shall retire," he murmured, lifting her hand to his mouth.

Rebecca giggled at his attempt at formality.

In one swift movement, Ray swept her against his chest, brushed his lips across hers in a tender caress and released her before she could even think to protest. Turning he picked up the tray and left the room, knowing that if he stayed a moment longer he would be called into account for his actions.

~*~

The next morning, Ray lingered in the shower after waking from a long, restless night. Too many memories had invaded his dreams, none of them good. *God*, he prayed in the silence of his heart, the depths of his soul. *Open my heart and mind, give me wisdom and direction. I really want to do something useful here and I really want to make peace with my parents. Even if it is only in my heart. There had to be something virtuous about them. Please help me to remember it.*

He dried off, put on his favorite pair of jeans, and slipped on a shirt without bothering to button it up. Some things just couldn't be contemplated before that first cup of coffee, he reasoned, bounding down the stairs in search of one.

The frustration of a sleepless night evaporated at the sight of Rebecca curled up on the couch, a cup of coffee on the table beside her, an open Bible in her lap. He stroked a hand down her hair. "Morning, Becca."

She smiled up at him. "Morning."

Ray grinned. "I didn't know you wore glasses." She lowered them a notch, peered over the rim.

"Only when I read."

He chuckled and pushed them up on her nose. "That's the kind of little things I want to know about you." He placed one hand on the arm of the couch and the other on the back. Boxing her into the corner where she sat, his lips brushed over hers in a tender caress.

She leaned into the soft cushions of the couch, placed her hand on his bare chest. Slowly, she spread her fingers and began exploring the different textures of his chest hair. He trembled at her touch. His heart thudded thickly, muscles jumped in reflex.

She closed her eyes, and he noticed the pulse throb in her throat. She wanted him as much as he wanted her. That made it difficult for him to pull away, but he knew he had to. She'd never forgive him if he allowed things to go too far.

He'd wanted only to kiss her good morning, but the gentle touch of her hand sent need spiraling like liquid heat through his body, galvanizing him in its wake. By the time she pulled her hand away, he was gripping the couch in a desperate attempt to keep from dragging her into his arms and cradling her against the chest she caressed so sweetly.

"Rebecca." He cleared his throat. "Look at me."

She lifted her gaze to his.

"I love you." Though he didn't expect a reply, the light in those smoky indigo eyes and the curve of her lips made his heart skip a thud.

"I want to hold you, Becca, but I'm afraid if I touch you I'll lose control and break the promise I made last night."

She swallowed hard, cradled his cheek in her hand. "I appreciate your control."

He moved his head so that his lips brushed across her palm in a brief, tender caress, then forced himself to move away without touching her. "Any coffee left?"

"Yes, and if you'll button up that shirt, I'll be happy to get you a cup." Her voice was thick, husky. Her gaze skimmed over his chest and lingered before returning to his.

He grinned, bit back a teasing retort that came to mind and winked. "You gotta deal."

Moments later she placed a cup in front of him. "What's on the agenda for today?"

Ray shrugged. "There's so much to think about, so much to do, I have no clue as to where to start. But I do have an idea. There's a little church not far from here that I occasionally attended while growing up. Want to go?"

A smile lit her eyes, curved her lips, and tempted him to taste her mouth. Ray settled for coffee, praying the sweet, creamy drink would suffice.

It failed bitterly.

"What time is the service?"

The question forced his thoughts into focus. "Ten." He glanced at his watch. "If we hurry, I have time to buy you breakfast."

Rebecca smiled. "If you're patient, we have time for me to cook us breakfast."

~*~

Ray enjoyed every moment of the Spirit-filled service. There was something solid and special, something cozy about sitting next to Rebecca, reading the Bible together in the quaint little church on the outskirts of town.

As the pastor began his sermon, a sense of peace and wholeness settled over him and he knew she belonged next to him. For the rest of their lives. He only hoped she felt the same way—that God had something bigger in store for their lives.

The preacher began to teach on the Sermon on the Mount and the Beatitudes, referencing other scriptures about giving to the poor and helping the needy. While he listened, Ray prayed for insight or direction on what to do with his parent's home and belongings. Several ideas presented themselves but only one took root and grew.

Chapter Sixteen

The ride home started out in peaceful silence.

"I know what I'll do with the house, Becca. I'll donate it to the city with strict instructions that it be used as a women's shelter." Ray warmed to the idea as he pondered it.

"That's wonderful. Do you think the neighbors will allow something like that?"

"The properties are far enough apart that I don't think it will be a problem. The area is zoned for multi- family—just look at all the guest houses around—and one thing my dad hammered into me was, 'son, you have to help those less-fortunate.' They stored up wealth and possessions, but they also donated a lot of money to the cause du jour."

Ray heard the snap of bitterness and took a deep breath to let it go. After all these years, it amazed him that the sting was still so sharp. Why had they cared for themselves, cared for others, more than they'd cared for him? He had to work past the pain. His parents were gone, and he needed to forgive them.

"The house is perfect for this. It's huge, fully furnished, and has a spacious, private back yard. It's in a neighborhood that's well patrolled and the house itself is protected by an extensive security system. Women and children can feel safe there. The study can be converted into a classroom where they can homeschool their children or further their own education, and the den can be modified into a play room for the little ones."

"You must have thought about this quite a bit."

"Not really. I've been praying for God to give me some direction. I feel in my heart that He's done exactly that. The idea came to me just this morning in church. And, the more I think about it, the more sense it makes. I don't want to live there. I never want to live there.

"Though abuse knows no boundaries, most battered women come from families like the ones you mentioned the other day—families who have struggled all of their lives for the bare necessities. They've never known anything else, never experienced anything good life has to offer. This place is a perfect haven for someone like that." He hesitated, wondering what Rebecca thought, how she felt, and was rewarded with one of her beautiful smiles.

"I think it's a lovely idea, Ray."

He grinned. "Me, too, and I want to make sure the director and counselors are all Christians, teaching the residents that through God's love and mercy they can experience the good things in life and that they deserve to live in a world where there's peace and blessing. Now, to figure out where to start."

"Open for suggestions?"

"Always."

"I'd suggest you start by calling your parents' attorney. He can probably answer all of your questions, especially about the legal aspects of doing this, and it's quite possible he can put you in contact with the people who can help you get the details worked out."

"You're right," Ray agreed. "Now I just need to decide what to do with all of my parents' personal things."

"Well, the first thing you need to do is get some boxes to pack them in."

He chuckled. "Right again." He circled into a store parking lot.

While shopping for containers, they discussed what to do with various items. The furniture, dishes, linens, and other such items needed to run a household would stay.

Ray would dispose of his father's things as well as go through his old room, and Rebecca agreed to sort out his mother's belongings.

Anxious to get started, Ray and Rebecca unloaded his purchases back at the house.

He'd bought plastic containers to pack up the things he'd get rid of and, at Rebecca's insistence, heavier ones for those he intended to keep—though he had no idea what that might be.

Standing in the living room with the plastic containers crowding the floor, Ray was overwhelmed at the task ahead. "I don't even know where to start."

"How about we start with lunch? I'll fix something and we can go from there."

Ray touched her arm. "Are you going to let me take you out at all while we're here?"

She smiled. "Of course, I'm looking forward to a nice, quiet dinner in a cozy little restaurant with you. But for now, I think we need a plan of action to accomplish the task at hand. Grab some paper and a pencil and we'll make a list of what to do and how to go about doing it. Nothing makes a job less overwhelming than being organized."

Ray agreed. He retrieved a notebook and pencil from his father's desk and joined her in the kitchen. Over lunch, they discussed all they needed to do. His father's clothes would go to a thrift shop, as would some of his mother's things. At

Rebecca's suggestion, Ray agreed to leave all of his mother's less-formal outfits for the women coming into the home, figuring some of them might be able to use nice clothes for job interviews and such.

"Jewelry, the crystal figurines, and personal mementos will be packed away for the daughters I hope to have someday," Ray said, warming to his theme. He looked up at Rebecca when he realized what he'd said, his heart plummeting.

A pretty blush heightened Rebecca's cheeks, but her brows were scrunched, and a look of worry replaced her normal joyous countenance.

"Adopted, stepchildren, or otherwise." He reached out and cupped her face. "I have no desire to wed a woman just to produce children. If we are blessed with them in any way, I will be happy, but I will be just as happy if God wills that we only have the two of yours and their future children."

Her expression cleared and she smiled, lifting his spirits.

The artwork would go to area libraries and museums.

Once the lists were made, he was anxious to get started. He was packing up the crystal figurines—as he'd been doing for hours—when Rebecca called to him from his mother's bedroom.

"Ray, can you come up here please?"

~*~

Rebecca sat on the bed with the contents of the little trunk she'd found. Her heart swelled with tenderness when she fingered the tiny christening gown, baby shoes and other mementos of Ray's growing up years.

Did he even know these things existed? Doubtful considering the resentment he harbored toward his parents. Rebecca prayed that showing him this would help heal the bitterness in his heart.

He stepped through the doorway as she closed the lid of the trunk. "Is something wrong?"

She swallowed hard, shook her head, and smiled. "Come sit here," she patted the bed beside her.

He grinned. "On the bed, Becca? Surely you jest?"

Rebecca rolled her eyes. "Behave yourself, Raymond."

He chuckled, sat beside her, and pointed to the trunk at her feet. "What'cha got there?"

"Look for yourself."

He eyed her, his brow arched in curiosity. Slowly, he opened the lid, as if the box contained something frightening.

Maybe it did.

A loud gasp escaped him as he lifted the tiny, white christening gown and with it, a picture of his parents on that day looking young and happy and very much in love.

"There's more," Rebecca said softly, rising from the bed. Taking the gown from him, she laid it where she'd sat and then lifted the trunk off the floor and put it beside him.

Tears filled his eyes, and his hands shook as he lifted the items and laid them across the comforter. His first pair of baby booties, shoes, a tooth, a lock of hair from his first haircut, his handprints on a paper plate that he'd given for Mother's Day when he was in kindergarten, a copy of the New Testament he'd given his mother as a teenager, a picture of every year of his life until he graduated high school. "I never knew about this."

Tears rolled down his cheeks. "I guess she really did care.

But why didn't she just say so?"

Rebecca tempered her words with care and compassion. "I don't know, Ray. Most mothers love their babies. She probably just got so caught up in the rest of her life that she didn't take time out to enjoy the gift God had given her when He gave her you. Maybe she forgot it was as simple as saying the words. Or could it be that a frustrated young boy, rebellious teen, or angry young man couldn't see the truth beyond what he was feeling?"

She softened her words with a smile as she picked up the tiny white gown. "Whatever the case, I'm sure she loved you. It's a sentimental soul that saves these kinds of things." She stroked the satin material, surprised at the quick spurt of longing in her heart for another child. She placed everything back in the trunk and closed the lid. "This is something you should keep and go through from time to time."

"I'll never make that same mistake." He grabbed her hand. "I love you, Becca. I hope you never get tired of hearing it because I'll never stop saying it."

His lips covered hers in a tender caress.

Within moments the trunk was on the floor, he was on his feet, and she was in his arms. Rebecca stiffened. "Ray, what..."

"I just want to hold you," he said in a soft, husky voice as he laid her on the bed and climbed up beside her. "Do you know how long I've wanted to hold you like this? I promise on everything I hold sacred that's all I'm going to do."

Rebecca ceased struggling at the intensity of his green gaze. "And what do you hold sacred, Raymond?"

"My love for you."

She melted. "Oh, Ray," she whispered, cupping his cheek

in her hand.

Triumph leapt to life in his eyes, curved his lips and escaped that lovely mouth in a satisfied little chuckle. Rebecca found she didn't mind when he wrapped her more firmly against his hard body, his hands leaving trails of fire where they caressed and lingered.

"Feels just right, doesn't it?" He snuggled his face in her neck. "You fit so perfectly in my arms."

Surprised at the truth in his statement, Rebecca trailed her hands over his back and shoulders, amazed at the comfort she felt nestled in his embrace.

"Talk to me, Becca. Tell me what you feel."

Rebecca opened her mouth to speak, flushed, stuttered, and then promptly shut it.

"Please, don't be embarrassed or ashamed."

"It's just hard to explain…. It's thrilling and yet, terrifying at the same time."

"You're not afraid of me, are you?"

Rebecca shook her head. "Not of you, of me, of this. I've never felt like this before."

Ray's mouth took a leisurely voyage across her face…. her lips, her eyes, her forehead. "I said I'd never want you to compare us with your marriage to Jim and I don't, but I am glad I make you feel something you've never felt before."

"Jim and I were both so young when we met." Rebecca's voice softened with nostalgia. "I was sixteen, he, barely seventeen. We shared the same foster home for a short time, and both wanted out—out of the home, out of the system. Both of us had been knocked around from pillar-to-post all of our lives and wanted nothing more than to belong–to something or someone, permanently. Then he turned eighteen, enlisted, and asked me to go with him. I was seventeen and figured marrying him was the only way to have a home and family of my own."

"Did you love him? Did he love you?"

Rebecca considered the answer, stretching her memory back to when she was a teenager. "Yes, we loved each other the way most teens do. Unlike most teens though, what we felt was more than just being infatuated with the idea of love, but the need to belong. By the time we realized life really wasn't all that easy, Jeff was on the way. Being from broken homes, we vowed to stick it out, no matter what.

"Eventually we grew to love each other with a more mature outlook. I never thought I could care about anyone the way I cared about him. Never thought I'd feel anything more than what we felt for each other. But, Ray, I care about you. And it's so different, so much more, that I'm almost embarrassed to talk about it, almost ashamed to admit it."

His grip tightened, eyes darkened. "Now that's something I won't allow. You have no reason to feel shame or even guilt. You loved Jim and were faithful to him. But, Becca, he's gone. That part of your life is over. I'm here now."

His voice softened. "I love you."

Rebecca shook her head. "But, surely it's wrong for me to feel so much more for you than I ever felt for him. He was my husband, yet I never wanted to touch him the way I want to touch you, to caress you, to feel you tremble beneath my hand. Why is it that I never felt that way about him? What does that make me?"

Raising her hand to his lips, he kissed the palm. "It makes you a woman, Rebecca, nothing more, nothing less than a beautiful, desirable woman with needs and feelings.

And there's not a single thing wrong in that," he insisted in an achingly tender voice.

"Touch me all you want," he whispered, placing her hand over his heart. "Feel what you do to me. And trust me, Rebecca. I promise I won't take this too far."

Rebecca closed her eyes, marveling at the way his heart thundered against her palm, matching rhythm with the blood thrumming through her veins. Mesmerized she slipped her hand inside his shirt, felt him shudder, and heard his soft moan of pleasure. Before she could jerk away, he covered her hand with his.

"It's all right. Don't be shy or afraid."

She lifted wide, pleading eyes to his. "But I am afraid, Ray. Afraid of where all this will end, afraid that I'll forget every scrap of morality I ever taught my children and even more afraid that I won't care if I do."

"I promise it won't go that far. I'll let you know when it's time to stop."

She allowed him to shift her slightly so that she was cradled against his side.

Murmuring soft words of love and praise, he urged her to relax and to trust him. Slowly, he unbuttoned his shirt and tugged it free from the waist of his jeans. Cupping her face in his hands, he covered her lips in a breathtaking kiss before pulling her into his arms once more.

As though in a trance, her hand moved across his chest to trace circles of fire over the sleek expanse of muscle and flesh. She felt him tremble, heard his sharp intake of breath and jerked her hand away, marveling that she was capable of eliciting such a response. It was obvious that by Jim always being the one to initiate intimacy between them, she'd been robbed of the simple pleasure of cuddling and caressing. And, oh, how she wanted to now.

When Ray didn't move or speak or open his eyes, she placed her hand over his heart once more. Propping up on one elbow, she ran her fingers up his throat, let them walk over his chin and sweep across his lips to cup one cheek as her lips brushed across the other. Rolling into a sitting position, she placed a hand on each of his shoulders and let them slide slowly and gently down his chest, thrilling at his soft groan of pleasure.

Ray grabbed her hands and stopped the sensual torture. "Now, Rebecca."

His voice sounded as though he'd swallowed a Brillo pad.

"We have to stop now, before there's no stopping at all."

He cupped her cheeks in his hands, pulled her across his chest and covered her mouth with his in a scorching embrace. The kiss ended on a groan of frustration when his lips left hers to travel across her cheek then forehead. Within moments, she was cuddled against his side once more.

"You have a beautiful body, Raymond." Her voice trembled with awe and wonder.

"From what I can tell yours is quite lovely, too, Becca." He took a deep breath. "What do you say we run over to the Y and take a swim?"

"I didn't bring anything to swim in, but you go ahead."

He wriggled his eyebrows with a mock leer. "That could prove quite interesting."

Rebecca rolled her eyes and flushed. "Maybe you should just take a cold shower, instead of swimming in a heated pool."

His reply was a throaty chuckle as he moved away.

Rebecca lay there for long moments after Ray rolled out of the bed and left the room. He returned a few minutes later carrying a duffle bag.

"Don't get up," he insisted when she moved to do so. Placing one knee on the bed, he leaned over and gave her a quick kiss. "Sure, you don't want to come along? My mother's bound to have at least one swimsuit in here that would fit you."

She shook her head.

"Want me not to go?"

Again, she shook her head.

He chuckled. "Cat got your tongue?"

She stuck it out at him.

He grinned. "See you in a while then." His voice was husky. "Love you."

He brushed his lips across hers once more then left.

Rebecca heard the door downstairs close and placed a hand over her still-racing heart. "God, what is happening to me?"

She couldn't recall feeling so alive, so consumed with emotions. With Jim, she'd felt a quiet sense of contentment, knowing she was loved and cherished, but she'd never thrilled to the point of having no concept of time or place, as she felt with Ray. She'd been too busy being a wife and mother to think about just being a woman.

Jim had worked hard to uncover that side of her, and she'd relished the times when he succeeded, but she'd never thought of herself as a sensual creature.

Until now.

Though she knew it was nonsense, she couldn't stop the quick spurt of guilt at the realization that Ray had only to take her in his arms and her whole body came to life. She wondered if the feelings would last when she was heavy with child or afterward when she was moody and grumpy and lactating. *What a ridiculous thought.* She hadn't even told the man she loved him. Yet here she was worrying whether or not the passion would last through pregnancy and parenting.

Rolling off the bed, she smoothed the covers then picked up the trunk that had started this whole episode. Opening the lid, she pulled out the christening gown and again felt a quick spurt of longing for another child. Smiling, she laid the gown gently on the bed, spread out the pictures of Ray and wondered what their child would look like.

Would he or she have her dark hair and his green eyes or his light hair and her blue ones? The questions made her think of her own children who'd both inherited dark hair and blue eyes from her and Jim.

Though he had the propensity for the breadth and width of his father, being an actor and dancer, Jeff tended to be long and lanky. Add a little fat to his diet and weight building to his exercise program and he'd be every bit as broad and muscular as his father had been.

Debbie had inherited the best of both of them, Rebecca's tiny frame, heart-shaped face, blue eyes and Jim's sense of order and purpose. Debbie would be a brilliant medical scientist one day.

Tears of loneliness and pain didn't close in on the familiar sense of pride in her children this time. Only pride and happiness. The worries about having another baby didn't outweigh the joy of that possibility.

Well, Lord, I guess this is Your way of showing me what the future holds, another marriage, and possibly more children. I gladly accept.

But the sensation that there was still more to His plan lingered in her soul.

Unwilling to disturb the atmosphere in the room. She walked out, closed the door quietly, and went to her room. After a quick shower, and dressing in comfortable jeans and a T-shirt, Rebecca went downstairs and started supper. She was putting the finishing touches on the table when Ray walked in looking lean and healthy and incredibly relaxed.

With the duffle bag tucked under his arm, a towel slung over his shoulder, his shirttail hanging out and his hair obviously combed only by impatient fingers, Ray's appearance was a far cry from his normal well-dressed attire. Still, the vibrant look of him stirred her sensibilities, and caused her hand to tremble as she lit a match and placed it to the wick of a candle.

He smiled. "Romance?"

"Ambiance," she countered. "Mood, atmosphere, tone."

He took a step closer as she blew out the match. "I know the definition of ambiance. Same difference if you ask me."

Rebecca turned as his arm slid around her waist. Even the strong smell of chlorine couldn't mask the musky scent of his skin. She placed a firm hand on his chest and felt his heart jump into high gear beneath it. A tremble skittered up her arm and down her spine. She shook her head, a tender smile curving her lips. "Supper's ready."

"Can I have desert first?" he queried in a soft, husky voice, his lips lowering toward hers.

Rebecca moved her head so that his mouth brushed against her cheek instead. "Absolutely not."

Ray chuckled. "Will it keep long enough for me to take a

shower?"

She nodded.

"OK, be back down in a flash." Ray bounded up the stairs.

When he came down again she waited at the table. He sat across from her and touched her hand. "Everything looks lovely, Becca."

She smiled. "Thanks."

Conversation remained light throughout dinner, and afterward when he pitched in to help her clean the kitchen. Both decided to forego any more packing, opting instead for a movie.

They returned late, aching from the sidesplitting laughter induced by the romantic comedy they'd chosen to view.

Goodnight was a tender kiss outside her bedroom door.

Though they laughed and talked, teased, and flirted, the rest of the week flew by without further incident. Watching God open doors for His will to be accomplished amazed Ray.

People not only accepted his idea of the house being used as a women's shelter, they approved it wholeheartedly. He donated the house and all its furnishings, as well as a substantial amount of money to get the shelter up and running. Within days, the arrangements were complete, and a director hired.

Ray's vehicle was loaded to the hilt with boxes of things he'd decided to keep or to give away as gifts to the few people enriching his life, and he found himself once again in the car with Rebecca. He'd cherished the alone time with her, and a seed of sadness crept into his heart at knowing things would be back to normal very soon.

On the trip home, they once again, traveled through Las Vegas. Rebecca threatened Ray with dire consequences if he even dared to mention a twenty-four-hour wedding chapel. They enjoyed an alternate route through Nevada, then California, which was no shorter than the way they took when they'd started their journey, but they enjoyed the quaint towns, cozy B&B's, and fresh seafood at dockside restaurants.

They arrived at Rebecca's house almost to the exact hour they'd left fourteen days before. A deep sigh reverberated through her. "Oh, it's so good to be home."

Ray unloaded her suitcase, frowned. "Yeah, except for the fact that now I'll be across town, and you'll be here instead of in the next room."

"No sulking." She patted him on the cheek. "You promised, remember?"

Ray couldn't help but chuckle.

She unlocked and opened the door. "Just put that anywhere, I'm going to go check on my plants."

Ray put down the suitcase and followed Rebecca when she hurried through the kitchen to the back porch, watching while she checked and watered plants, and grinning at her sweet murmurings as she did so. "You talk to your plants?"

Rebecca smiled. "Yes. It's good for them. Haven't you heard talking to plants makes them grow better?"

He shook his head. "I learn something new about you every day, and the more I learn the more convinced I am that I've given my heart to the right woman."

Rebecca laughed as he slid his arm around her waist. "And like I've said before, you are an incurable flirt. Would you like a cup of coffee or something?"

Ray grinned. "What I'd like is to be invited to sleep on your couch. I don't know if I can stand being in my great big apartment all alone."

She shook her head. "Big? Your apartment is not even half the size of this house."

"It's huge when you're alone," he murmured, lowering his lips toward hers.

Rebecca's giggle escaped against his mouth. "Tell you what, I'll fix us some dinner, and we'll watch a movie, but then you have to go home."

His mouth twisted into something between a grin and a frown. "OK."

She eyed him for a moment. "And no pouting or sulking or pulling that 'too tired to drive' excuse, either."

Ray chuckled. "Now, Becca, do you think I'd pull such a stunt?"

She laughed. "You're a man aren't you?"

Chapter Seventeen

Rebecca stuffed gift bags for Halloween. As always, she included pennies for blessings. Taking a deep breath, she looked around, pleased everything was ready for the horde of children that would come trick-or-treating. As she'd done every year, she prayed over each gift-bag, asking God's protection on the children and their families.

A knock on the front door startled her out of her deep concentration and prayer. She walked to the living room and glanced out the window, surprised to see the young Korean man from before. She opened the door. "Hello."

He smiled. "Hello. You said I come back."

Something about him tugged at her heart. Rebecca nodded. "How've you been?"

"Good."

She stepped back from the door and smiled. "I'm glad to hear it. By the way, I'm Rebecca. What's your name?"

He grinned, reminding her of how young he was and of her own children living away from home. "My name Jin."

"Excuse me?"

"Jin. As you say, G-e-e-n."

"Oh, *Gene.* Good to know you. Would you like something to drink or eat?" She led the way to the kitchen.

"That be nice. You busy?" He waved to encompass the decorations and gift bags on the table.

"Sit." Rebecca pointed to a chair. "Just getting ready for the children who'll come for treats. Do you do Halloween in Korea?" She retrieved two glasses from the cabinet then opened the freezer to collect ice for their drinks.

"No, no Halloween. We celebrate Chusok."

"Chusok?"

Jin smiled. "A festival where we bring rice and fruit offerings to our ancestors in thanks for the results of their labor."

Rebecca poured them each a glass of fruit punch. "Oh, kind of like Thanksgiving here."

Jin nodded.

"Sometimes I think we Americans have too many holidays. But it's fun for the children and I love them all."

"You like children?"

Rebecca nodded, then placed Jin's drink in front of him and took a sip of hers. "I love children. I wanted a whole houseful, but Jim insisted we stop at two. Said that's all we could afford to raise properly and send to college."

Brimming with love and pride, she snatched a photo of her and Jim with Jeff and Debbie off the refrigerator and held it for him to observe.

Jin reached for the photograph, hesitated, wiped his fingers on his pant leg and then gazed at the family portrait.

"Nice." He set the photo on the table. A tiny smile tugged at his lips. Taking a deep drink of his punch, he glanced into her face as an awkward silence filled the room. He rose from the table. "Well, guess I should go. Thanks for the drink."

Rebecca wondered at his sudden silence but didn't question. She picked up a gift bag filled with treats and handed it to him. "Here you go, enjoy. Come back again."

She led the way to the front door, watching as he left. Before she made her way back into the kitchen, there was another knock on the door. Thinking it may be early trick-ortreaters she rushed to the kitchen and grabbed a couple of gift bags then hurried back only to find Ray standing on the porch.

They'd been back from Flagstaff for two weeks, and he'd yet to return to work. She talked to him nightly, saw him nearly as often, and they'd planned on him being here this evening, so it shouldn't have surprised her that he arrived early.

"Trick or treat," he said when she opened the door.

She held up the bags and arched an eyebrow. "Which would you prefer?"

"Treat of course, but not that kind." He slid his arm around her, his lips capturing hers in a brief, tender caress.

"You're here early."

He grinned. "Came to protect you from all the ghosts and goblins."

She laughed. "But they won't be here for hours."

"And your point might be?" he asked with a chuckle.

She shrugged, shook her head, and headed toward the kitchen.

Following Rebecca, Ray took a deep breath and inhaled the aromas filling the house. "Man, this place smells wonderful. My stomach is growling, and my mouth is watering."

He reached for a cookie. "These look great."

Putting the gift bags back with the others, she slapped his hand away. "They're for the children."

"Aw, c'mon, Becca, surely you have at least one extra."

He sounded every bit like a sulky six-year-old. Rebecca relented and handed him a cookie.

"Ummm, a man could get used to this much sweetness."

Though the words indicated he talked about cookies, his eyes said something completely different.

"Too much sugar is not good for you," she countered, as he took a step nearer and blocked her in against the table.

"When are you going to just give up and marry me, Becca?"

"Who says I'm going to marry you at all, Raymond?"

He regarded her with laughing green eyes. "'Cause that's the order of things."

Rebecca rolled her eyes. "I'm almost afraid to ask, but what do you mean by that?"

He grinned. "First comes love then comes marriage then comes Becca with a baby carriage," His voice mimicked that of a mischievous child.

She giggled. "You've missed half of the nursery rhyme."

"I don't see how you figure that. There's been plenty of the k-i-s-s-i-n-g and the tree part can be arranged."

Before she could even consider the implications of that statement, he swung her into his arms and tossed her over his shoulder like a sack of potatoes and headed out the back door.

"What are you doing?" she shrieked between giggles. "Put me down."

"Can't. Gotta find a tree."

Every ounce of dignity Rebecca tried to summon was lost as the giggles increased. "But what will the neighbors think?"

"Probably that we've lost our minds." He stopped just below the lowest branch of a huge tree in her back yard. "Here we are," he said, maneuvering her around so she could grasp the branch. "Up you go."

Unable to do anything else, Rebecca grabbed the branch,

scrambled onto it, and continued to laugh.

He jumped, got a hold on the limb, and scooted up the tree until he was seated in front of her. "Man." He sighed, shook his head. "I've never had to work this hard for a kiss."

His faux complaint threw her into another fit of giggles. Rebecca continued to laugh while he inched toward her until their bodies almost touched. Before she could catch her breath from laughing so hard, he scooted another notch closer and cupped her cheeks in his hands.

"You're an idiot." She grabbed his wrists, breathless from exertion. "A one hundred percent, USDA prime idiot and I love you Raymond Jacobey."

Ray rolled his eyes and grinned. "Now she tells me. All the cozy dinners, romantic movies, and late night calls, and she tells me while sitting in a tree in the back yard."

He chuckled. "I love you too, Becca. Now"—his voice lowered a notch— "let's see if I can get this right."

He began to sing. "Ray and Becca, sitting in a tree, k-i-s-s-i-n...." each phrase, each syllable, was punctuated by a teasing caress of his mouth against hers.

By the time he finished the rhyme, Ray had her cradled against his chest with one arm. He slid the other around her and pulled her closer.

Ending the kiss by slow degrees, Ray eased her back against the tree trunk, grasped it with both hands to keep them from tumbling off and buried his face in her neck.

"Now, Becca, any more nursery rhymes I need to learn or obstacles I have to overcome before you agree to marry me?" He pressed his lips to where the pulse beat madly at the base of her throat.

Rebecca slid her hands up the firm wall of his chest to

cup his face. "No more obstacles, but I would like you to meet my children first."

His lips traveled up her throat, over her chin and covered hers in a tender caress.

"But you will marry me?"

"Yes, I'll marry you."

"Even if they don't approve?"

"It's not their approval I'm seeking. I'm not worried about that. They'll love you as much as I do. It's out of respect that I want you to meet them first. I wouldn't want either of my children to marry someone I hadn't met. It's only fair I abide by that principle myself."

"Can we have a baby of our own?"

The intensity of his green gaze sent goose bumps shimmering up her spine. "I'd love to have another baby, Ray. God willing, it'll be yours."

He jumped down off the branch and reached for Rebecca. She slid into his waiting arms. He held her close for a moment and brushed his lips across hers in a tender caress. "You've made me one happy man, Becca."

Keeping one arm around her waist, he walked with her back into the house.

They spent the rest of the evening laughing and talking and serving treats to the assorted miniature ghosts and goblins, aliens, and angels, as well as the celebrities and politicians coming to her door.

Chapter Eighteen

Rebecca tiptoed past the couch where Ray slept, on her way to the kitchen. In the week since she'd agreed to marry him, he'd been a constant guest, sleeping on her couch on more than one occasion. Usually, the sight of him stretched out there made her smile. Today she frowned.

Time for him to go home.

She cringed, surprised at the vehemence of her own thoughts. Her hands trembled as she turned on the coffee pot then checked and watered her plants. When she finished, and the coffee was done, she poured herself a cup and plopped down in a chair at the table. The strong, hot brew did little to ease the chill in the air much less the one in her soul.

The beauty of autumn with its warm, golden leaves had been lost when November blew in with fierceness, bringing with it freezing temperatures, rain and snow. Rebecca stared out the kitchen window oblivious to everything but the gray sky and the ache in her heart. An ache brought on by...what?

She shook her head and tried to figure out exactly why she was in such a foul mood. Taking a deep breath, she closed her eyes. The moment she did, memories and visions of her dreams the night before filled her mind, the clarity of which caused a frisson of need to curl in the pit of her stomach.

Maybe it was because she was happy and content. Maybe it was because Jim's kiss didn't affect her the same way Ray's did. Rebecca felt the familiar spurt of guilt at that thought and wallowed in it for a minute before shoving it aside. Maybe it was because she'd been alone for over a year and was just lonely. Whatever the reason, the need was great.

And it was all Raymond's fault.

Ever since that kiss in the tree, he'd been the perfect gentleman. His kisses were light and friendly, not once getting out of hand, which only seemed to add to her exasperation. She never dreamed she'd be tempted to forget every scrap of morality she'd worked so hard to instill in her children.

She glared up as the object of her frustration ambled into the kitchen looking well-rested and incredibly sexy. His sandy-colored hair was tousled, and a day's growth of beard shadowed his cheeks, but his smile was as bright as the light in his eyes.

"Good morning." He reached for a cup and poured himself coffee.

She glared at him and grumbled something unintelligible.

"Guess not, then. Coffee?"

She shook her head and placed a hand over her cup.

He put the pot back on the warmer, picked up his mug, walked over to the table, and stroked a hand down her hair. "Is something wrong?"

"I didn't sleep well."

Ray trailed his lips across her cheek. "Sorry to hear it. Is there anything I can do?"

"Go home."

"What?"

"I need some time alone. I'll fix you some breakfast. Then it's time for you to go home."

The temperature in the room lowered another degree. "You mean like 'don't call me, I'll call you' go home?"

"I didn't say that."

"No, not in those exact words, but everything about you is screaming at me. What's wrong? Unless I'm mistaken everything was fine when we went to sleep last night, so what's going on?"

"I just told you. I didn't sleep well. I'm asking you to respect that and go home so I can get some rest."

The coffee suddenly tasted like ashes in his mouth. Ray spun back to the sink and dumped it out, angry at the quick stab of fear and insecurity that pierced his heart. "Don't bother with the breakfast, Rebecca. I get the hint. I know when I'm not wanted around. Known it all my life."

She pushed back from the table with such force, the chair nearly toppled. "Oh, please, don't give me the poor, mistreated-little-boy attitude. When this whole ordeal started, you promised you wouldn't sulk or pout if I said I needed some space. That's all I'm asking for here."

"It's more than that." He strove to keep his voice calm. "You glared at me when I walked in the kitchen, grumbled when I said good morning, and froze up when I tried to kiss you. Now I want to know what is wrong."

He lowered his voice a notch. "Besides, I thought we had more than just an 'ordeal'."

Rebecca pressed her fingers to her eyes then rubbed her temples. He reached out for her, trying to figure out what had made her so angry, but she stepped back.

"Don't touch me. I can't think when you touch me. I just need to be alone for a little while. I told you I didn't sleep well last night. I'm in a bad mood, and I just want you to leave me alone."

Ray felt the rejection like a slap in the face. "Fine, Rebecca. If that's the way you want it, I'll leave."

He marched into the living room, tugged on his shoes, and slammed out of the house. He'd gotten to the top porch step when he realized he didn't have his keys or wallet. They were still on the coffee table where he'd put them last night. He rotated on his heel with a muttered oath and went back inside. The sound of her sobbing ripped at his heart. Unable to bear it, he walked back into the kitchen and pulled her in his arms despite her protests.

"I thought you left!"

"I did. I had to come back in and get my wallet and keys." He ran his hands up and down her back in a soothing gesture. "Talk to me, Becca. Don't shut me out. You want to scream and fight, we'll scream and fight. You want to take a swing at me then take your best shot. Whatever it takes. Just don't shut me out."

"I don't want to scream and fight." She raised clenched fists to his chest and pushed out of his embrace. "I just can't stand this tension!"

"What tension?" He shook his head, confused. "I don't know what you're talking about." Another look had him backing up in consideration.

Her face was flushed, taut, her eyes fierce. Clenched into tight fists by her side, her hands trembled. "I've never been so frustrated in all my life."

Desire erupted in him with volcanic force, galvanizing in its wake. Ray swallowed hard and clenched his fists to keep from reaching for her.

She's practically begging you to take her to bed, a little voice in his head taunted.

A powerful need to take her in his arms swept over him but Ray hesitated when she buried her face in her hands and wept. *God, help me! I'm only human here. Give me wisdom. Tell me what to say. Show me what to do.*

You know what to do, the little voice sneered. *Be a man.*

Sheer force of will stopped Ray from responding to that little voice and doing what he wanted—take her in his arms and love her until neither of them could think, move, or breathe without the other. What he didn't want were the regrets and recriminations that would follow if he ignored not only her but his values, as well as God's command to be holy and abstain from sexual immorality.

But you love her, the voice jeered. *You've waited for true love all your life. How can it be wrong? How can it be immoral?*

Ray shook his head to quiet the voice of his flesh and pleaded with God for guidance, understanding, something. An unnatural calm enveloped him and by divine revelation, he understood—even if Rebecca didn't—that her frustration stemmed from the need to be held, cuddled, loved, and from unrelieved desire.

A need he had exposed. A need he shared. With a silent prayer for strength and self-control, he reached for her. Keeping his voice low and gentle, he said, "Come here, Becca."

She shook her head and took another step back. "No, Ray. I..."

He closed the distance between them and cupped her cheeks in his hands, cutting off her protests. "I'm just going to hold you," he whispered, his lips brushing over her forehead in a tender caress.

"That only makes things worse."

"It won't. I promise. Let me show you. Let me hold you."

When she didn't refuse, he swung her up in his arms, carried her into the living room and settled on the couch with her cradled against his chest.

Gentle fingers tangled in the thick mass of her hair while his lips caressed her forehead, eyes, mouth, and cheeks. Rebecca remained stiff and tense despite the tenderness of his embrace.

"I love you," he whispered. "Intimacy doesn't always mean ending up in bed." He saw the skepticism in her eyes and kissed them closed. He stroked her back and shoulders. "Relax. Trust me."

His arms remained gentle, his voice soft, and his words tender as he whispered husky endearments of love and adoration.

Tears welled in Rebecca's eyes and rolled slowly down her cheeks. "I don't understand what's happening to me."

Her voice, hardly more than a hoarse whisper, sent an ache clear to his soul.

"There's nothing wrong with needing to be held, Becca. That's what I'm here for. Can I ask you something?"

He hesitated when she stayed silent and continued when she nodded. "Was your husband affectionate?"

She stiffened. Ray hurried to calm the demons of doubt before they took root in her mind. "You don't have to answer if you don't want to. I'm not trying to judge him, you, or your marriage. I just want to know where our similarities and differences lie."

"I'm not sure I know what you mean by affectionate."

Ray chuckled. "What I mean is, was he a touchy, feely kind of guy?"

She smiled and shook her head. "Not like you. He was gentle and kind. I always knew he loved me, but he wasn't as demonstrative about it as you are."

"Does that bother you?"

"It never has before. But I guess it does bother me to think something was missing in our relationship."

"Having it now doesn't mean something was missing in your relationship. I've said it before. I'll say it again, I don't ever want you to compare our love to the one you shared with Jim. But please, don't ever fear talking to me. I want to know how you feel, what you're thinking. If you just need to be held or want to be cuddled, ask. It's a sure bet I'll ask it of you when I have the need."

"Jim never was the cuddling type. Unless you consider holding hands to be cuddling. He was always gentle and showed his love in a number of ways, but when he took me in his arms, it usually led to sex. I guess that's why I'm so afraid of it now. Afraid of where it will all lead. Afraid that I'll get so caught up in the joy and pleasure of it that I won't care if we end up there."

Not wanting her to feel the desperation of his own need, Ray forcefully kept a tight rein on his emotions when he kissed her. "Not all men are the cuddling type. My father wasn't. Neither was my mother for that matter. The one thing I yearned for the most as a child was to be held and loved and adored. That's what I always thought love was all about, how it should be expressed.

"I don't want you to fear this between us. I know how you feel about pre-marital sex and I feel the same way. But Becca, holding and cuddling doesn't always have to end up in a sexual encounter. That's where self-control comes in." He took a deep breath, gathered his thoughts, and continued.

"Even the Bible talks about expressing love in tender caresses, passionate embraces, pretty words. I know it's meant to demonstrate God's passion and love for the church, but I believe it's also there to demonstrate to men and women what we need from each other and what God intended for relationships, especially marriages to be like.

"Just because Jim didn't see it that way doesn't mean he was wrong or that your marriage was lacking. There's no doubt in my mind that your husband loved, honored, cherished, protected, and provided for you. You were happy, content and committed. That says a lot about your relationship. It means a whole lot in this day and age when, for so many people, love is just a four-letter word with no substance to it. My love is not meant to be a measuring stick for you to judge between Jim and me. It's only meant to show you another side of tenderness, another definition of affection. Please don't think less of what you shared with Jim just because I have a different way of showing you how I feel than he did."

Rebecca lay in his arms. As he spoke, he could feel her tension drain away. When her breathing deepened and body went lax in his arms, he held her while she dozed. She jerked awake. Ray cupped her cheek in his hand, pressed her face into his shoulder in a tender hug. "I love having you in my arms, Becca."

"I love being in them, Ray."

"Isn't this much better than fighting or being alone?"

She nodded. "Can I ask you something?"

"Anything."

"Have you decided if or when you're going back to work?"

He grinned. "Why? Are you getting tired of having me underfoot?"

"I'm just not used to having someone around all the time."

He laughed. "I'm not sure. I've thought about it, but as much as I enjoyed my job, this is the time of year I always dreaded, the cold, the rain, and the snow. And now that I really don't have to work…"

"But what will you do with yourself all day?" She lifted her head and looked at him, obviously horrified.

His grinned at her with mischief. "Anything I want."

He rolled to his feet and offered her a hand-up. "You still want me to go home?"

She smiled, ran her fingers through his hair. "Yes, but not for the same reasons."

"OK. When can I come back?"

Rebecca smiled, and he was relieved to see she felt better.

"The door is always open. Now, how about some breakfast before you go?"

"I'd love some." He followed her into the kitchen.

Chapter Nineteen

Thin along the edges, a deck of high-altitude clouds faded from dark gray in the west to pale almond near the east. Behind the mountain peaks sunbeams reached up to embrace the billowy fluffs, creating a pink tinge that highlighted the massive rock formations like halos while turning them the color of rich cream.

Rebecca gazed out the window of her front door, amazed at the glorious display of light and shadow. *If only I had a camera.*

She knew, scientifically, the gorgeous scene before her was sunlight reflecting off moisture in the clouds. Rebecca preferred to think of the stunning sunrise as an exhibition of God's art. She also knew the presentation would only last a few minutes, and would disappear as the huge, red-gold orb continued its climb heavenward. So, she stayed put and sipped her coffee as the brilliant hues bled away like someone throwing water on a beautiful painting.

Rebecca finished her coffee, put down the cup and stretched while rubbing her lower back. For the past four days, she'd done nothing but clean cabinets, closets, dresser drawers, and floors.

Ray had been out of town for nearly a week, and she'd used that time to begin sorting through the remainder of Jim's and the kids' things. Though they hadn't discussed it, she imagined she and Ray would live here once they married, or at least until they found a home of their own. The thought made her smile and think about the upcoming holidays.

Thanksgiving was less than three weeks away, Christmas break, six. Six weeks, and her kids would be home for two. Fourteen delightful days jam-packed with love, laughter, and chaos.

Sheer bliss.

Rebecca could hardly wait. Not only for the arrival of her children, but the joy and blessings that would follow. Perhaps this time next year, she'd have a new baby at her breast. Her heart sighed, the pleasure of the idea chased away the momentary doubts and fears.

She closed her eyes and let the wonder and anticipation of what was to come envelope her, wrapping her in a cocoon of warmth and light rivaling that of the sunrise she'd just witnessed.

God, her soul whispered. *I never thought I'd feel this way again. Not since those days when I first fell in love with You.* Her whole being sang with joy and thanksgiving of His goodness and mercy.

"Thank You," she murmured, exulting in the glory of His presence then she sank to her knees and raised her hands in praise.

Her intimate encounter with the Holy Spirit was all too brief, but its residual effect followed Rebecca throughout the morning and into early afternoon while she resumed cleaning and sorting through years of accumulated belongings. That was exactly what she was doing when a knock sounded on her door. She opened it to be greeted by a now-familiar face.

Jin smiled. "Hello."

Rebecca returned the greeting. "How've you been?"

"Good."

She stepped back from the door with a smile. "C'mon in. Would you like something to drink or eat?"

"Thanks."

Asking his preference of tea, Rebecca set about preparing them each a cup as well as a sandwich. They ate in silence for a few minutes.

"Last time I visit you talked about your two children?"

Rebecca nodded, remembering. "Yes, I showed you a picture of us all."

"Where are they?"

"My daughter is in France going to college. My son lives in New York. What about your family, do you have any siblings?"

Jin frowned. "What sibling?"

"You know, brothers or sisters."

Jin shook his head a hint of sadness clouding his eyes. "No sibling. My mother home in Korea, my father deceased."

"Oh, I'm so sorry to hear that. How did he die?"

"I not sure, my father American. I not know him well. Only met couple times. He die before I could know him."

The thought of this child not knowing his father brought back memories of her own childhood, and Rebecca felt a surge of kinship with him. "I never knew my father either. He died before I was born. My mother died when I was four and my grandparents whom I lived with, died when I was six."

"Who raise you?"

"I was raised by strangers. In the welfare system."

Jin shook his head. "I not understand. What welfare system?"

"A government program for orphaned children."

"You have no more family?"

Rebecca shook her head. "Not that I know of. I had a grandmother, my father's mother, but I never knew her. I don't even know if she's alive or what."

"Sad," Jin said. "I have my mother and grandparents. They die a few years ago, just me and mother now."

"It must be hard being away from her."

He nodded. "Yes, very hard, especially since she sick. I wanted to stay in Korea with her, but she insists I come to school in America. I hope to find my father when I come, but not possible now."

"You said you saw your father a couple of times. If so, then you must know his name. Does he have any other family?"

Jin looked at her for a long moment. "He have other family. I don't think they know about me."

Rebecca's heart constricted when she thought about what this young boy was going through, alone in a strange country, the only family he had probably not even aware of his existence. A knock on the door sounded before she could think of a suitable response. She rose from the table.

"Excuse me." One glance at the clock brought a smile to her lips. She took a moment to run her fingers through her hair before making her way to the front of the house.

Rebecca opened the door and jumped into Ray's arms, scattering mail all over the porch. "I missed you!"

Laughing and breathless, she rained tiny kisses all over his face. "I never thought I'd miss you so much!"

The five days Ray had spent in Flagstaff sorting out more of his financial affairs had been some of the longest of her life.

Ray laughed, picked her up and twirled her around then

captured her lips in a thorough embrace. "I missed you too," he said, his voice something between a groan and a chuckle. "We made a mess of things."

Rebecca followed his gaze to the fallen envelopes all around them. A self-conscious little giggle escaped as she squatted to pick them up. Scent wafted up. Rebecca raised the envelopes to her nose, inhaling the fragrance from the stickers. She blinked back tears. "Oh, Ray, you remembered."

"How could I forget?" He gave her a tender smile. "You looked so adorable when you said that you missed them. I couldn't get your expression out of my mind the whole time I was gone."

Ray helped her gather the remaining envelopes, stood, and offered her his free hand. She accepted it, rose, and led the way to the kitchen. "C'mon in, there's someone I'd like you to meet."

Ray frowned. "Who?"

She glanced back over her shoulder at him and smiled. "A new friend."

As they entered the kitchen, Jin rose from his seat at the table.

"Ray, I'd like you to meet Jin. Jin, my friend, Ray."

"Meeting you nice."

Ray reached out to shake hands. "Likewise."

Jin shook Ray's hand then looked at Rebecca. "I should go."

Rebecca smiled, took him by the arm, gave it an affectionate squeeze, and escorted him to the front door. "It was so nice to visit with you. Come back again. Anytime."

Jin smiled at her. "Thank you."

Rebecca waited until he'd stepped off the porch before

she closed the door and returned to the kitchen.

"Is he the kid you told me and Jeff about?"

She smiled. "Yes, and as you can see, he's totally harmless."

Ray chuckled and took her in his arms, covering her lips with his. "I missed you." He nibbled at the corners of her mouth.

His teasing sent tiny sparks of pleasure through her entire being. She slid her arms around his neck. "I missed you, too."

Her lips reached for his once more.

Ray put one arm around her waist and buried his other hand in her hair and ended the kiss by slow degrees. "I love you."

"Love you, too." She slipped from his embrace. "Tell me about your trip."

Ray shook his head. "Not much to tell. Got some more details ironed out on liquidating everything and making sure the shelter has plenty of money at least for the first year or two or until they can get set up for grants and such. Reinvested some money for our future and moved some into my accounts here. Tell me about this Jin kid."

Rebecca told him what she'd learned about Jin's life. "It's so sad. Being so far from home, no family left except for his mother who is still in Korea and an American family who probably doesn't even know he exists."

"Did he tell you his family name?" Ray seemed uneasy, but Rebecca discounted it as his protective streak.

She shook her head. "No, we didn't get around to discussing it. He'd only been here a few minutes when you arrived."

"It must be difficult not knowing who you are or where you came from."

Rebecca didn't miss the innuendo in his words. She closed her eyes and took a deep breath. "You think I should open that letter, don't you?"

Ray covered her hand with his. "Don't you think it's time to make peace with your past?"

His tone was gentle, but she got the message and glared at him.

He laughed. "And don't you hate it when your own words come back to haunt you?"

"Yes, I do." She reached for the cigar box that had sat on the table since the early September morning when she'd received the letter. Her hand trembled as she opened the box and took out the envelope. Her heart thundered as she removed the contents and unfolded the letter.

Dearest Rebecca, it is my hope I am still alive when you read this. It's also doubtful that I will be, as I find myself getting weaker by the day. Either way, please allow an old woman a few moments of your time to pour out her heart in apology and repentance for denying you your birthright and the chance to grow up within the haven of family. But you see I was bitter and angry at the loss of my son. And though I couldn't deny your existence and how much you resembled your father, I could deny you were his.

Alas, I know now, even as I knew the times your mother brought you here, that you are most definitely my granddaughter, and I regret not ever taking the time to know you, to love you, and to give you the opportunity to know your father through those who loved him more than life itself.

My man at the investigation agency has been searching for you for more than twenty-five years now. The constant moving during your years in the foster care system then your husband's Air Force career, made the search long and difficult as these types of records are not always available to the general public, especially since you never showed an interest in finding us. For which I don't blame you.

No matter the reason, I've found you now. It is my prayer that you'll forgive an old woman's ignorance and selfishness and come to Hammondsport. Please know, I will harbor no ill will toward you should you decide not to. However, the door is always open.

Your inheritance waits.

Her grandmother's name, signed in a weak scrawl that Rebecca could barely make out, triggered a whirl of emotions in her heart. Elizabeth Mae Rawlings, her grandmother, her flesh, and blood. Tears dripped down her cheeks when she handed the letter to Ray.

"All these years," she mumbled. "All these years, and I never knew."

Ray skimmed the contents then folded the paper, slid it back into its envelope and laid it on the table between them. "Her middle name is Mae. My mother's name was Regina Mae."

Rebecca smiled at the awe in his tone. "We should carry on the tradition, if we ever have a daughter."

Ray grinned. "I like that idea. So, want to go or not?"

"I don't know." She inhaled a sharp breath. "Do you think I should? I mean there's no date on the letter. Maybe I should call or write first."

"Looks like an open invitation to me. I think we should

book the next flight out and just go. Wait a minute." He picked up the letter again. "You said lilacs and grapes?"

Rebecca nodded.

"They're not in season at the same time. In fact, your grandmother says the 'times' your mother brought you there. So, you had to have gone more than once."

Rebecca shrugged. "Maybe. I don't really remember."

"Tell me about the dream. Leave nothing out."

Rebecca closed her eyes. "I'm driving up a long, winding road. There's a glint of silver in my rear-view mirror. The scent of lilacs and grapes are heavy in the air. So heavy in fact, I can smell them now."

"Was your husband ever stationed near Hammondsport, New York?"

Rebecca shook her head.

"Then you couldn't have been driving. Weird."

"I know."

Ray shrugged. "Oh, well, it'll probably make sense once we get there."

He scooted back from the table and walked to the counter to get the phone. Within a few minutes, he'd booked the next flight out. They would land in Rochester then rent a car to travel to Hammondsport. Their departing flight would leave in less than four hours.

Rebecca packed a suitcase, called her children, and took a shower. She and Ray stopped off at his apartment on the way out so he could repack his suitcase. Since layovers would put them in Rochester sometime in the early morning hours, they would rent a car, find a motel for the remainder of the night, and then travel on to Hammondsport the next day. To what, Rebecca didn't know. Would her grandmother still be alive?

Chapter Twenty

Located on Route 54 at the head of Keuka Lake, Hammondsport was less than two hours from Rochester.

Still, Ray lingered over the drive, stopping several times to enjoy the view and scenery. Though he'd slept very well, he could tell by the look of her, Rebecca hadn't had a peaceful night.

He paused on a hilltop and rolled down the car window to gaze at the valley below. Ripe with scents, the air had a bite to it. Where Washington seemed frozen in time, this part of New York was milder, welcoming. Fall clung tenuously in rich, vibrant leaves that refused to succumb to the cooler temperatures and strong winds determined to rip them from the trees. The smell of freshly picked grapes mixed with wood smoke from chimneys invited the mouth to water and stomach to grumble.

Ray decided whatever awaited them in Hammondsport could wait another half-hour or so. He pulled in at a quaint little cafe in a tiny community along the way. Taking Rebecca's cold hand in his, he lifted it to his mouth. "Hungry?"

Rebecca shook her head. "Not really."

"Scared?"

"Terrified." A visible shudder followed her soft reply.

"Terrified of what?" Ray wanted to know when she lifted a trembling hand to tuck a stray strand of hair behind her ear.

The gaze she leveled at him held a kaleidoscope of

emotions, a glimmer of excitement, a hint of worry, a shadow of fear.

"Of what I might find...or more like, what I might not find."

"Whatever it is, it can't be all bad, Becca."

Rebecca only shrugged.

"How about a bite of breakfast, or at least a cup of coffee?"

Taking her silence for acquiescence, Ray got out of the car and walked around to open her door.

An hour later, she still pushed the food around on her plate and her coffee had grown cold.

Ray lifted her chin with a gentle finger. "We don't have to do this. We can turn around and go home if you want."

Rebecca leaned back in her chair, closed her eyes. "You probably think I'm such a coward."

"I'd never think that of you. But, I feel as if I pressured you into coming here without giving you time to think things through and to know if it's what you really wanted. So now I'm offering you the chance to go home and do so."

Rebecca smiled. "You're so sweet. I just don't know what to expect. What if she's still alive, can I ever forgive her? And if she's not, will there be any evidence of love, or anything left of my family? She said my inheritance waits, but what does that mean? What inheritance?

"All I remember was a big house—huge if my memory serves me right. But, like I said, I was only a child. It may not be big at all. Regardless, what will I do with it all?"

"You're thinking too far ahead. Look at the bright side. Consider the possibilities. Suppose she is alive. Don't you want the opportunity to at least meet her and find out something about your father and the family you should have known? And, if she's not, from the tone of her letter, I'll bet there are plenty of things to provide that link for you—photos, family documents...Think about the future and not the past. Suppose when we get married, we move here instead of staying in Washington. Consider the location. You're only about, what, six, maybe eight hours away from New York City and Jeff. Debbie is just an ocean away instead of clear across the United States *and* the Atlantic. But still, don't fret over it all. Let's just get there and see what we find, and we'll handle circumstances as they arise."

Rebecca sighed. "You're right. I guess I am being silly."

Ray chuckled, interlaced his fingers with hers and kissed the knuckles. "You're not being silly. You're just borrowing trouble. Remember what the Bible says about not being anxious for tomorrow, because tomorrow has enough problems of its own. Let's get there and see what we find."

Rebecca tugged their joined hands to her cheek and rested her face against them. "OK. Let's do it."

Thirty minutes later, they climbed the hill into Hammondsport.

A tiny, Victorian town which appeared to be stuck somewhere between one century and another lay spread before them. Nestled among busy streets were cobblestone sidewalks, village square shops and quaint little antique stores.

Ray pulled into a parking area near the Post Office and walked inside to get directions.

~*~

Located ten miles north of town, the drive was all uphill. A glint of silver caught her eye. Rebecca glanced in the mirror. Rays of sunshine bounced off the lake and unleashed a flood of memories. "It wasn't paved roads back then," she remarked, her mind's eye replaying that trip so long ago.

"What else do you remember?"

Rebecca closed her eyes and let the scenes wash over her. "It was cool. Not hot like Texas."

"That's where you grew up?" She nodded and opened her eyes.

"Where in Texas?"

"A dozen different homes in twice as many towns and just as many counties. The one thing Jim was adamant about while in the Service is that he never be stationed in Texas. Once we got out of there, we never wanted to go back."

Ray smiled over at her. "It was that bad?"

She shook her head. "Not really, I guess. But when you're young and alone like we were, you grow to hate the system, and to us, Texas was the system."

"Well, let's not think about that. What else can you remember about your trips here?"

Taking a deep breath, Rebecca closed her eyes once more and searched her mind. "The windows were down. I stood next to mama while she drove. I remember looking into the rearview mirror and seeing the sunshine reflected off the water."

A smile crossed her lips. "Like it is now. The smell of lilacs was so strong in the air. I can still see the pretty purple flowers. We did come twice because the next time it was a lot cooler. Mama had the windows up and the heater on in the car. But when we got out, there were grapes as far as the eye could see. I remember mama telling me to smell the grapes and how pretty the scent was."

"Do you remember what month it was?"

She shook her head. "Not really. Why?"

"Well, the scent would be much stronger during harvest time and that's around October. It would be pretty cool then, too."

"Makes sense." Conversation halted as Ray maneuvered the car onto the long, winding drive which led up to a huge, two-story Victorian.

"Wow. It's gorgeous."

Rebecca shivered. "It's cold and impersonal."

Ray chuckled. "That's my line."

She smiled at his attempt at humor and watched while he disembarked from the vehicle, walked around to the passenger side, and opened her door. He took her hand and guided her out of the car.

They stood a moment, awed, and stunned.

Unkempt grapevines, tangled with briars and brambles, marred the beauty of the landscape. A closer look at the house revealed peeling paint and patches of rotting wood. Making their way to the porch, Rebecca gasped in surprise at the meticulously kept lawn behind the rusty gate that separated the yard from the vineyards.

"May I help you?" A voice came from the side of the house.

Rebecca turned as what appeared to be a gardener or groundskeeper approached. "I'm looking for Elizabeth Rawlings."

The man shook his head and sighed. "Too late, we buried Ms. Rawlings four days ago."

The quick jolt of regret tugging at her heart surprised Rebecca. "Well, can you tell me where to find the executor of the estate?"

"In town. Lawyer by the name of McQuarkindale."

"Thank you." Rebecca turned to go.

"Uh, Ma'am?" The query halted her decent. "You wouldn't happen to be Rebecca, would you?"

She faced him once more and nodded. "Yes, I am. How do you know about me?"

"Your grandmother talked of you often. She wanted so badly to meet you. Sorry she didn't live long enough."

"So am I," Rebecca murmured, surprised at how true those words were and the wave of grief that accompanied them. "Can you tell me how to find this Mr. McQuarkindale?"

"Back down the hill to Hammondsport. Turn left at the first light. His office is on the right about three places down. You'll see the sign."

"Thank you."

"But if you want a key, I have one for you."

Rebecca waited while he fished a key ring out of his pocket and removed one from it. He held it toward her. Her hand trembled when she took it.

He turned to leave.

"Wait! I didn't get your name."

"It's Tim, Ma'am."

"Are you the caretaker?"

Tim nodded.

Rebecca held out her hand. "Well, thank you, Tim, for everything."

"What'll you do with the place, Miss, Rebecca?"

Rebecca shrugged. "I don't rightly know yet. This is all

so new to me." She gasped. She had all but ignored Ray the whole time. "Oh, I'm so sorry. Tim, this is Raymond Jacobey, a friend of mine."

The two men shook hands, and then Tim addressed Rebecca. "Well, you'll find the family cemetery just behind the cottage out back. I'll be around in the morning to collect the key and maybe by then you'll have some idea what you're going to do."

Rebecca reached a hand toward him. "Tim?"

He turned.

"Is my father buried in the family cemetery?"

He nodded.

Rebecca blinked back tears. "Thanks again. We'll see you in the morning."

With another nod, he turned and left.

Rebecca unlocked the door with trembling hands. It opened with an obstinate squeak. She stepped through the doorway and stood in awe at how immaculate the inside was compared to out. Oak paneling lined ten-foot walls. Exposed beams supported cathedral ceilings. A wrought-iron staircase led to the upper floor where they found more of the same. A balcony at the front of the house led outside onto the widow's walk. Elegantly furnished in priceless antiques, every room held a plethora of memories. Pictures, photo albums, diaries, and journals lined shelves in each room. She could read for days and barely scratch the surface of history surrounding her family and the estate.

"This would make a magnificent B&B," Ray remarked, as they made their way down the back stairs and into the kitchen.

Rebecca nodded. "I was just thinking the same thing."

Opening the back door, they walked onto the wraparound porch and gazed at the Victorian cottage snuggled in an alcove of trees not two hundred yards behind the house. A stone walkway led straight to its front entrance. The same key that unlocked the main house opened the cottage.

Once again, they were astounded at the elegant beauty that greeted their eyes upon entering the building. What appeared to be no more than a tiny cabin was actually an exquisite home containing three bedrooms, two baths, a living room, dining area and kitchen.

Ray turned to Rebecca. "Are you thinking what I'm thinking?"

She laughed. "Depends on what you're thinking."

He chuckled. "That this would be perfect for us, and that we could turn the big house into a bed and breakfast."

"My thoughts exactly," Rebecca admitted with a smile. "Let's go visit Mr. McQuarkindale and see what he has to say."

The meeting with Mr. McQuarkindale lasted longer than they expected, so Ray rented them each a room at a local inn.

The next morning, they drove back to the estate to return the key to Tim before heading back to Rochester to catch a flight home.

Walking through the house once more, Rebecca gathered several of the diaries and journals to read in the days and evenings to come. "There's one more thing I'd like to do before we leave."

He smiled and tucked a stray curl behind her ear. "The cemetery?"

She nodded.

"Let's go then." They picked their way through the

overgrown grass and weeds behind the cottage and walked up the hill to the family plots.

Hesitant, Rebecca leaned on the rusty gate barring the entrance to the cemetery.

Ray waited silently and stroked a hand down her hair. "Want to go in?"

She shook her head. "It's not something I want to rush through, and we need to go. I just wanted to walk up here for a minute."

"We'll make the time if you want."

Again, she shook her head. "No. This is fine."

A few minutes later, she smiled up at Ray, took his hand in hers and walked back to the car.

The trip to Rochester and the flight to Washington were filled with snatches of conversation interspersed with long stretches of companionable silence.

Rebecca glanced through the latest journal her grandmother had written, amazed at the wealth of emotion it contained. Grief, sorrow, and love, all woven together in a beautiful tapestry of prose penned by the hand of a woman who, by the grace of God, had changed from an angry, bitter soul to a gracious and loving lady.

Chapter Twenty-One

The next few weeks passed in a flurry of activity. Faxes and phone calls between Rebecca and Mr. McQuarkindale were constant until the estate was settled. The cottage would be scrubbed and painted and ready for her and Ray to move into the first week of January.

In the course of probate and succession of her grandmother's estate, she discovered that one of the local wineries had leased the vineyards until a couple of years ago and arrangements were made for them to resume the tradition. The winery would once again care for, cultivate, and harvest the grapes as they had for centuries before, providing a substantial income.

She and Ray agreed to tackle the main house once they moved and settled into the cottage.

Instead of just cleaning and sorting through her current home, Rebecca packed things to be shipped to New York.

Ray also packed up his belongings, bringing the boxes over to Rebecca's to be stored with hers until time for them to leave.

During one of those hectic days, she welcomed the diversion when Jin showed up for a visit. She prepared them each a cup of hot chocolate and told him about the letter she'd received and her trip to New York.

"So, you move to New York?"

"Yes. I can hardly wait either. Ray and I are going to get married and live in the cottage, and then we're going to turn the big house into a bed and breakfast."

"Guess I won't see you anymore."

Rebecca heard disappointment in his voice and covered his hand with hers. "I'll still be here through Christmas and the first of the year. You're more than welcome to come back."

He shook his head. "I go home for Christmas."

"Well, that's good. When do you leave?"

"December twentieth."

Rebecca laughed. "Really? That's the day my kids are coming home. Do you need a ride to the airport?"

Jin grinned. "That be nice. Maybe I meet your kids."

Rebecca shrugged. "Maybe. What time do you leave?"

"Eight o'clock in the morning."

Rebecca shook her head. "They don't get in until eight-forty-five. But I don't mind taking you to the airport."

"Thanks."

On a surge of maternal compassion, Rebecca hugged him. "It's been so nice meeting and visiting with you, Jin, and I really hate to rush you off, but I've got a ton of things to do today. What are you doing for Thanksgiving?"

"My sponsor family wishes I stay with them."

"Sponsor family?"

He nodded. "I part of foreign exchange program."

"Oh. Well, that's good then, you won't be alone. Wait here, I've got something for you." She rushed to her bedroom and retrieved a picture of her, Jim, and the kids. Returning to the kitchen, she handed it to him. "Listen, if you never meet your American family, we'd be honored to call you a member of ours. If you're ever in New York look me up."

She wrote down the address in Hammondsport and gave

it to him.

Tears filled Jin's eyes. He reached for both with trembling fingers. "Thank you. I honored, too." He hugged Rebecca and left without saying another word.

Thanksgiving came and went, Rebecca and Ray shared frozen turkey dinners while continuing to sort and pack.

Christmas quickly approached, but with Ray's help, Rebecca took time out of her frantic schedule to put up a tree and decorate the house.

Communication with the kids was sparse and sporadic as each wrapped up their perspective lives in preparation for the holidays at home. At last, December twentieth arrived.

Rebecca waited in the airport terminal watching for her children. She spotted her son's head above the crowd, and bit her lip to keep from crying out until they were within hearing distance. She waved to get their attention. "Jeff! Deb!"

"Mom!" they shrieked in unison, bolting through the terminal gate to sweep her into a group hug.

"Oh, you both look so wonderful!" Rebecca gushed, laughing, and crying all at once.

"And just look at you." Jeff twirled her around. "Why, you're practically glowing."

"And you cut your hair," Debbie exclaimed.

Rebecca ran her fingers through the short tresses.

"We've been so busy I found myself tucking it up into a hair clip or ponytail so much I got frustrated and lobbed it off."

She laughed. "Had to go to the salon and have it shaped, and I'm still not used to the new style. But it's growing on me. Ray loves it though.

"It looks wonderful," Debbie assured.

Jeff agreed. "Where is your hero?" he asked, winking at his sister.

Rebecca laughed and draped her arm through his. "My hero is at home, his apartment rather, waiting on a call. He thought we'd like some time alone, and graciously offered to give us a few days before meeting you. As long as I called to let him know everyone made it in safely."

"That's mighty nice of him," Jeff said.

Debbie giggled and slipped her arm around her mother's waist. "How is Ray, Mom? Is he as cute, sweet, and sexy as I remember?"

"Deborah!" Rebecca admonished, heat scorching her cheeks.

Debbie eyed her mother, her brow lifted in curiosity. "Well, is he?"

"More than you can even begin to imagine," Rebecca confided in a loud whisper.

"Oh, please, you two That's more information than I want to know so spare me the details. Have you been waiting long?"

Rebecca laughed at her son's statement. "Actually, I've been here since before eight this morning."

Jeff frowned. "Why so long?"

"I brought a friend to catch his plane at eight and as you know, we had to get here early."

"A friend?" Deb asked her eyebrow arched in interest.

"Yes, a young Korean man. He's about your age or somewhere in between you two." Rebecca paused, realizing she really didn't know as much about Jin as she'd like. "Anyway, he was going home for the holidays, so I offered to bring him this morning. We visited while we could then I drank a ton of coffee and haunted the gift shops while waiting for you two."

"Is that the same kid you've been telling me about?"

Rebecca caught the note of irritation in her son's voice. "Yes. But before you get all bent out of shape, Ray has met him and agrees he's as harmless as a tadpole."

She smiled at her son and raked her fingers through his hair as she had when he was little. "He's just a lonely kid, Jeff. I merely offered him a bit of friendship."

She hugged both of her children. "Oh, we have so much to talk about! I have so much to tell you, I don't even know where to start."

"How about the beginning," her daughter teased, setting the tone for the next few days.

Deb and Jeff retrieved their luggage, and then the three made their way to the parking garage and found Rebecca's car. Jeff loaded everything, and they headed home where a full course meal consisting of their favorite dishes awaited them.

During the course of the evening and over the next few days, Rebecca told her children the story of her inheritance and her plans for the future. Discussions were lengthy and emotions sometimes ran high when she met with opposition from her son.

Always one to keep the peace, Debbie sided with her mother against his most vehement arguments.

"I can't believe you're just going to pack up and move clear across the country on a whim. What does this Ray guy have to do with this?" Jeff asked.

"Ray is behind me one hundred percent. He thinks it's a great idea."

Jeff shook his head. "I don't understand how you can do it. This is your home. How can you just leave it?"

Rebecca eyed her son. "Isn't that what you did? Run off to follow your dream, to fulfill your destiny? What would you suggest I do with the rest of my life— sit around and waste away while waiting on you and Deb to come home when you have the chance?"

"No, but..." Jeff hesitated then shrugged. "I don't know. It just seems like a big jump from one life into another. What makes you think you can run a business?"

"What makes you think I can't? Managing a Bed and Breakfast isn't much different than running a household. It's what I've done all my life. It's what I like to do, what I'm good at."

"Why don't you just sell everything and enjoy life for a change. Travel around, see the world. Why do you want to saddle yourself with something like this?"

Rebecca sighed and rubbed her throbbing temples. They'd been at it for days. "It's what I want to do. I'm not one to live frivolously or impulsively. I have to have purpose in my life. This business gives me that. Besides, it'll bring me closer to you and Deb and maybe we can see each other more often."

Debbie walked into the room. "C'mon you guys, give it a break. It's time to call a truce."

Jeff scrubbed the heels of his hands over his face. "You're right."

He slipped his arms around his mother. "I'm sorry. Whatever makes you happy makes me happy."

He grinned, the charming, roughish grin he'd inherited from his father and used on her for years. Rebecca tugged on his ear. "Thank you. The last thing I want is to spend the rest of the holidays arguing with you, especially when all the opposition in the world won't make me change my mind."

Christmas Day dawned bright and clear. Ray arrived on Rebecca's doorstep thirty minutes early. Though he talked to her nightly, not seeing her the past four days had been torture. He knocked on the door and waited for someone to open it, surprised when that someone turned out to be a tall, lanky, young man. He smiled. "You must be Jeff."

Jeff nodded, one hand on the door, the other cradling a cup of steaming hot coffee. "I am. And you must be Ray."

Ray chuckled. "I am. Where's your mother?" He'd barely gotten the words out of his mouth when she came rushing down the hall, past her son, and into his arms. She squealed his name and laughed as he enveloped her in a bear hug.

"Morning, Becca." He pressed his lips against her mouth.

Ray didn't miss the look Jeffrey sent his sister as he mouthed, "*Becca?*"

Debbie grinned and joined them. "Hi, Ray. How are you?" She reached out to hug him.

Ray accepted her embrace. "I'm fine. Good to see you again."

"Good to see you too. C'mon in."

The day passed without much incident as did the next two. Consumed with the holiday spirit, Rebecca was stunned to walk out back three days after Christmas to find Jeffrey and Ray in a heated argument. She stopped and listened when the two men went nose to nose, snarling at each other.

"What do you mean, I'm being selfish?" Jeff demanded.

"That's not what I said," Ray countered. "I said that I believe you're thinking more about what you want, instead of what your mother needs."

"Means the same thing if you ask me! Besides, what makes you think you know what my mother needs?"

Ray shook his head. "Because I love her, and I want to marry her."

Jeff snorted. "Marry? Are you crazy? She doesn't need to get married. She needs to live a little, not be tied down in another marriage! She just escaped from one hellhole; she doesn't need to get caught up in another one."

Ray stiffened. "What do you mean by hellhole? I thought she and your father were happy."

Jeff grunted. "That's what they wanted everyone to believe. But I know better. He wasn't happy, didn't want anyone else to be happy either. That's why I got out of here the day I turned eighteen."

"What exactly are you hinting at? Spit it out," Ray demanded.

"My father was selfish and self-centered. A control freak who made our lives miserable. She was just too naïve or blind to see it."

"Maybe she loved him too much to dwell on his faults," Ray argued. "Or maybe she loved you and Debbie too much to think of leaving. Especially with her, their, upbringing."

Jeff snarled. "Maybe she was just too afraid of what he might do to her if she ever considered leaving, and, on top of everything else he was a liar and an adulterer!"

"What makes you say that?"

"Because he told me. He's got at least one bastard kid in

Korea!"

The shock on Raymond's face mirrored that of her own as every ounce of warmth seeped from her body. Rebecca stormed between them and turned on Jeffrey in an angry whirl. "How dare you say something like that about your father?"

"Because it's the truth, Mom. And I don't want to see you go through that again. I can't believe you're even thinking about getting married after what he put you through."

"You're overstepping your boundaries, Jeffrey."

"Well, someone needs to! You're out of your mind!"

"Jeffery, that's enough! Go into the house, I'll deal with you later."

She turned to Ray when Jeff stormed toward the house.

"Becca, I'm sorry."

"Why are you even talking to him about this? My marriage, his father, is none of your business!"

"He was being unreasonable."

"He's a kid compared to you!"

"He's a grown man!"

She held up a hand. "I don't want to talk about it, Raymond. Just go home."

"Becca..." his words trailed off when she turned away. "You're not being fair."

She whirled on him. Her fists clenched with the effort it took to control her emotions. "Fair! I come out here and find you quarreling with my son, and you have the nerve to say that I'm not being fair?"

"Look, I don't know where, when, or how this all got out of hand. I only wanted to talk to Jeff about us getting married. Call me old-fashioned or whatever, but I thought it'd be nice to ask him for your hand. I'd hoped to get his blessing!"

Rebecca rubbed her temples and fought down the sobs threatening to overtake her at any moment as Jeff's words, slung about in careless anger, set off a trembling of emotions in her heart and soul.

"Please just go home, Ray. I don't know what to think about this whole mess. I'm too upset to even think! I need to be alone."

"I'm sorry," he whispered. Turning, he did as she asked and took his leave out the back gate.

Rebecca's heart felt as though it were splintering into a thousand jagged pieces. Bile clogged her throat when Jin's image rose in her mind. His visits took on a whole new meaning as each replayed in her memory. Unspoken words, innuendos, and unanswered questions, rolled around in her head until she thought she'd be sick.

She stumbled to her room, threw herself on the bed and sobbed. Shattered. Heartbroken. Broken into little bitty pieces. No way to glue it back together. She had no idea how long she stayed there until Jeffrey appeared by her side.

"I'm sorry, Mom. I'm so sorry." He put his arms around her, choked on a sob. "I didn't mean to blurt that out. I'd never want to hurt you that way."

"How did you get in here?" She knew she'd locked her door!

He held up a tiny crochet hook. "Dad kept it on the top of the door frame, in case one of us kids locked ourselves in."

Another aspect about Jim she'd known nothing about.

"How do you know about...about...this child?"

"He told me the night of my seventeenth birthday. One of

his famous 'life lessons'."

Rebecca heard the bitterness in her son's voice and cringed. "Does your sister know about this?"

"I don't think so."

"Well, I don't want her to know. Not a word! At least until I can figure out what to do about it. Do you understand?"

Jeff nodded.

"I still don't understand how you could have known it all these years and I never had a clue. I thought I knew you. You're my son. He was my husband. I don't know either of you anymore!"

"Please don't say that. I love you. I was just a kid. I didn't know what to do with the information."

"But that was years ago. Why couldn't you have told me at some point since then?"

"What was I supposed to do? When—how was I supposed to tell you that?"

"I don't know. I'm so confused and hurt and angry right now I can't even think straight."

"I know you are, Mom, and I'm sorry. It shouldn't have come out like this. We'll talk all you want, but not right now. You don't want Deb to know and neither do I. She's going to be back from skiing anytime now, so let's just let it go for now. We'll talk all you want later."

Rebecca allowed her son to help her to her feet. She took a long, hot bath and went to bed, unable to face her daughter until she'd had a chance to pull herself together. It didn't help that her sobs continued deep into the night, as she clutched her pillow and wondered about the fantasy that had been her life for the past twenty-plus years.

Chapter Twenty-Two

Rebecca did her best to make the last few days of her children's visit as festive as possible. Though a strain, she managed to keep her emotions in check. At least during the day. Nighttime was a different story. Many times, she went to bed with sorrow in her heart and tears on her pillow.

Before anyone was really ready to say goodbye, December thirty-first arrived.

On impulse, Rebecca packed a couple of suitcases and accompanied her children to New York. She and Jeff waited at the airport with Debbie as long as they could. When the time came for her to go through the security check, Jeff hugged his sister.

"Take care of yourself, kiddo."

"I will. Take care of you." She gave him a tight squeeze and glanced between him and Rebecca. "And whatever is wrong between you two, please don't wait too long to straighten it out. Life's too short."

Debbie hugged Rebecca, tears streaming down her cheeks. "I love you, Mom. Are you sure you're going to be OK? I can skip a semester and stay with you."

Rebecca sniffed back tears and swallowed the lump in her throat before answering her daughter. "No. You can't. I won't allow it. I'll be fine, sweetie."

Debbie gazed at her for a long moment then nodded. "OK. Take care of yourself and promise you'll be happy. You always taught us to follow our dreams, now it's your turn. Don't miss out on a single gift life offers you."

Rebecca hugged her daughter. "I love you too, Deb, and I promise. Call as soon as you get on the ground, no matter what time, so we'll know you made it back safe and sound."

Amid hugs and kisses, they said their final goodbyes, and then Debbie stepped through the security check.

Jeffrey put his arm around Rebecca's shoulders and hugged her to his side. "Let's go, Mom."

She let her son lead her out of the airport and to his car but waited until they were safely ensconced in his apartment before confronting him for the last time. "We need to talk."

"I know. I have no idea where to start. So, you ask the questions and I'll answer them as best I can."

"You said your father told you about this child on your seventeenth birthday. What exactly did he say?"

Jeff hesitated a moment, took a deep breath and enveloped her hands in his. "The first thing he told me was how he met and fell in love with a beautiful girl when he was my age."

She smiled.

"Then, he asked me to understand that he was young and didn't know the Lord back then. He said he'd met the woman in a bar. Some soldiers were harassing her, so he stepped up to stop them. They became friends, and one thing led to another. Six months after he returned home, a fellow airman contacted him. Seems the girl was pregnant. She'd told him all about Dad and swore he was the father. Blood tests confirmed it."

With mixed emotions, Rebecca listened to the story of her husband's infidelity. How could something so life-changing be that simple? Be relayed in a matter of moments, with so few words? "That's all? That's the whole conversation?"

Jeff nodded. "That's the condensed version."

"I don't want the condensed version. I want the details. All of them."

Jeff sighed. "He did say that when he initially returned home, he regretted his indiscretion and vowed to never make that mistake again. He also insisted he'd never been unfaithful to you after that, even the times when he returned to Korea. However, he did live up to his responsibility toward the child by sending money to the mother."

"So, you knew the first time Jin showed up that he was probably your father's child?"

Jeff visibly cringed at the accusation in her statement. "I suspected. But when you told me you'd run him off that first time, I figured he'd never return. And I hoped I was wrong about his parentage. Then when he did come back and you told me that Dad had been kind to his mother, I started to put two and two together. Still, I hoped I was wrong. I considered telling you while I was home, but once I got there, I had no idea how to go about it. Nor did I think you'd befriended the kid so that he'd keep coming back. Then, the thought occurred to me that maybe he would tell you, and I could play dumb about the whole thing. The coward's way, I know. But I had no idea if, when or how I should tell you. I certainly didn't mean to blurt it out like I did, Mom, and I'm truly sorry."

The prick of betrayal rose in her heart but was soon surpassed by compassion for her son. After all, he'd been a child when he learned his father's secret. In many ways he still was. *He was her child.* A deep, long look into his eyes told Rebecca more than words ever could. "You've held this against your father all these years, haven't you?"

Tears welled up then rolled down his cheeks. He nodded as deep, shuddering sobs began to shake his whole frame. "I was so angry. I couldn't wait to leave. To me he was just a big hypocrite, spouting Bible scriptures and talking about the Lord when all the time he was lying to us. Lying to you. A sin is a sin and a lie, even the lie of omission, is still a lie."

Rebecca put her arms around her son and rocked as she had when he was younger until his sobs changed to soft, hiccupping sounds. "Not forgiving is as bad as the rest, sweetheart."

"I know, but by the time I got out in the real world and realized how complex life could be, it was too late. I never got a chance to say I was sorry and that I forgave him."

"Have you laid this at the feet of Jesus, Jeff, and asked Him to forgive you and heal you of the bitterness, anger and guilt?"

"I've tried. But I couldn't really accept His forgiveness or forgive myself as long as I knew I was as bad as Dad for not telling you. Can you ever forgive me?"

Rebecca hugged her son. "Oh, honey, you're my son. I'll always forgive you. I may not understand your decisions or actions and I may not agree with them, but I'll always love you and I'll always forgive you. I have one other question..." She hesitated.

"What about the other things you said about your father? That he was selfish and self-centered, that he was a control freak and never really happy. Did you mean those things or was it anger and bitterness talking?"

Jeff took a long moment before answering. "A bit of both."

Rebecca's heart sank at her son's words. She knew he and his father didn't get along so well those teenage years and after, but figured it was the normal behavior of a boy becoming a man. How could she have missed the deeper reasons? Did she not know her son or husband at all?

Jeff shifted in his chair and rubbed the back of his neck. With a heavy sigh, he continued. "True, he was controlling and liked order, but he was never really abusive. But there always seemed to be an air of discontent about him. Like he was never satisfied, or truly happy. Of course, that could be because he knew he should tell you about this kid. What's his name again?"

"Jin. I appreciate your honesty. Even if it is a bit late in coming," she added with a smile and hoped Jeff knew he'd been forgiven, completely and unconditionally.

~*~

The next morning, Rebecca rented a car and drove to Hammondsport. There, she buried herself in grief, letting the gamut of emotions run their course. Anger and betrayal ripped at her heart and mind until all that remained was sorrow, shame, and an overwhelming sense of failure.

Although she'd loved Jim and tried to make their marriage work, she hadn't succeeded in making her husband truly happy. Something had always been missing.

Even though she knew now what that something was, she still didn't know if he'd died with regret or unhappiness in his heart. And if she'd failed him, she wondered, how on earth could she ever hope to make Ray happy?

For two weeks, the icy New York weather matched the

chill in Rebecca's heart. She sat at the kitchen table within the warmth of the cottage and nursed a cup of coffee. She hadn't talked to Raymond in all the time she'd been gone. Instead, she'd spent many sleepless nights plagued by doubt, insecurity, and unanswered questions. She thought about him constantly, torn between calling and leaving him alone. Many nights of tears, followed by prayer and Bible reading helped her come to terms with what she'd learned about her husband, but she still had no idea of what to do about Ray. She'd left things with him so undone, and now, knowing her marriage hadn't been the stronghold she'd thought all these years, she was even more insecure.

"Oh, God," she murmured, overwhelmed with a sense of loss and sorrow. "What now? What have I done? What am I going to do about Ray? I miss him so much." But could she marry him knowing she might not only disappoint him but be completely clueless to the failure?

She closed her eyes, swallowed the hard lump of emotion clogging her throat, and let the tears come.

She heard the rattle of the mailbox then a knock on the door. Unwilling for the letter carrier to see her in such distress, she waited until he left before she got up to see what he'd delivered.

She lifted the envelopes out of the box and caught a whiff of fragrance. Turning them over, she saw why. Scented stickers covered the entire backside of every envelope.

"Oh." She gasped, covering her lips with trembling fingers. Hope flared in her heart. Tears streamed down her cheeks as she looked around.

"Ray?"

Sensing rather than hearing a movement, she spun as he

slipped up behind her. "Ray!"

She flung herself into his arms and sobbed into his shoulder, soaking his shirt with happy tears. "What are you doing here?"

Ray swept the hair away from her cheeks. "I told you when we first started this relationship that I'd never give up and I'd never let you go."

"I'm so sorry. I owe you some sort of explanation and an apology but so much has happened. I don't even know where to start."

"Let's go in. It's cold out here."

Once they were settled at the kitchen table, each with a cup of coffee, he ensconced her hand in his, raised it to his mouth and kissed the palm. "You don't have to tell me anything. Jeffrey called and told me you were here. He also apologized and gave us his blessing."

"Did he tell you about his father's secret?"

Ray nodded. "I didn't want him to go into detail since your marriage to Jim is none of my business—you were right when you said as much—but he insisted on telling me so I would understand his initial reaction to us getting married."

He sipped his coffee. "I told you a long time ago I never want to compare our relationship to your marriage with Jim. But, Becca, I do want you to know that I will never cheat on you. You don't have to worry about that. Nor do you have to concern yourself that I'll keep or hide things from you. I know Jim may have had his reasons, and I'm not judging him. But I believe in complete, open honesty between a husband and a wife. In fact, I insist on it."

Tears coursed down Rebecca's cheeks at the unconditional love pouring forth from him. Still, she was so afraid. She rose from her seat and refreshed their coffee. "I'm not sure I can marry you."

"What?"

The fear and insecurity in his eyes tore her heart out, but she had to be honest. "I'm not sure I can marry you. It took all of this for me to realize I'd failed Jim. I never made him truly happy. I'm afraid I'll fail you too."

"That's nonsense. How did you fail him?"

"As much as I tried to make him happy, there was always a sense of discontentment in him. The kids felt it, too. Well, at least Jeff did. You've never been married. You have no idea the situations that can come up between a husband and a wife. I'm not sure I want to go through that again. Or even if I should."

"So, you're saying we're through?"

Rebecca swallowed the tears clogging her throat and took his hands in hers. "I don't know what I'm saying right now. I only know I could never forgive myself if I made you unhappy."

Ray raised their hands to his mouth and looked her in the eyes. "I doubt anything you could do or say would ever make me unhappy. As far as I'm concerned, Jim is the one who failed. You are a beautiful, loving, generous woman. You remained honest and faithful. Jim failed you, Becca. You promised you'd marry me, and I refuse to let you finagle your way out of that promise with these silly ideas of being a failure."

He rose, pulled her up out of her chair, and put his arms around her waist. "Not only will our marriage be a huge success—because, lady, I plan on making you deliriously happy the rest of our lives—but our B&B will be successful.

And the women's shelter will flourish."

He brushed his lips over hers in a tender gesture then continued. "Now, no more of this nonsense or I promise, I'll hog tie you, throw you in the backseat of that rental car, and force you to marry me. Oh, and, you'll be gagged, too."

Love and laughter shone in the teasing green gaze, fueling the hope that had flamed in her heart from the moment he showed up on her porch. A smile tugged at the corners of her mouth. "What makes you think you can get away with that? I have a son, you know, and though he may be half your age he's every bit a grown man."

Ray nodded, grinned. "What makes you think he'd take your side in all this? Especially since I've already gotten his blessing to marry you. Besides, he warned me you might have some reservations about remarrying."

"Oh, he did, did he?"

Ray nodded. "Yep, figured you'd be sitting up here blaming yourself for things you had no control over and told me not to let you get away with it."

Rebecca couldn't stop the thrill of pride in her son. "I guess my Jeff is growing up."

Ray pulled her against his chest. "Takes after his mother," he murmured as his lips covered hers in a thorough caress.

Epilogue

At Jeff's request, Rebecca and Ray flew to New York City to be married.

Though she and Ray discussed a no frills wedding, Rebecca was surprised and pleased at the effort her son put into ensuring the opposite. Her dress reminded her of fairytales and happily-ever-after endings.

The ceremony and reception were no less mystical. Since Debbie could not attend, Ray suggested they delay the honeymoon until the spring when they could travel to France during Debbie's semester break.

After a blissful weekend in the suite reserved for them, the newlyweds flew to Washington to finish packing, ship what they could, and to rent a truck to transport the rest of their belongings back to Hammondsport.

In the course of the long flight and equally long layovers, Rebecca and Ray discussed what to do about Jin.

Since she'd been robbed of knowing her father, Rebecca was determined not to make the mistake her grandmother had.

"You can't blame the child," she told Ray, to which he agreed, saying once again that he'd given his heart to the right woman.

When Jin showed up at her house three days after they arrived, she opened the door with a smile. "Hello, Jin Sinclair."

He paled, and then flushed. "You know?"

Rebecca nodded. "I know. And I thank you for having

enough consideration for my feelings that you kept the truth from me. But, as it turns out, my son knew of your existence. His father...” her words trailed off as the realization that Jim was also Jin's father hit her with full force.

Her heart trembled nearly as much as the hand holding onto Jin's. She swallowed hard, grateful when Ray slipped his arms around her waist. “I mean, your father told him of the relationship between him and your mother. And of you.”

Shock, worry, fear, flitted across Jin's features. “Does he hate me?”

Rebecca's heart went out to him. She smiled, gentle peace flowing through her. “No, he doesn't hate you. He's still a bit angry and confused, but he doesn't hate you.”

She silently promised herself to have a nice long talk with Jeffrey to ensure he also would not blame the child for the ill-conceived choices of their father.

Tears filled Jin's eyes. He blinked them back. “I'm glad you and he know. Mother insist I not betray your kindness by telling you the truth. She be happy to know all is well.”

“How is your mother?”

He shook his head, the tears escaping. “She die while I home.”

Rebecca felt his grief as though it were her own and pulled him into her arms, grateful when Ray embraced them both. “I'm so sorry.”

“And n-now y-you l-leave...” he sobbed.

The weight of her decision warred with her emotions, tearing at her mother's heart. But Rebecca knew she couldn't change her entire life for this one child. “Yes, I'm leaving, Jin. But you'll always be welcome. I gave you my New York address, do you still have it?”

He nodded.

"Good. I'll write as soon as we get settled, and I'll give you our phone numbers. Ray and I are flying to France to visit with my daughter"—Again, she hesitated, the knowledge that Debbie was his half-sister filling her with mixed emotions. Her vow to not blame the child reiterated itself in her mind, grace filled her soul, love ruled her heart. She smiled— "your sister, and while we're there, I'll tell her about you."

"Do you think she hate me?"

"No one will hate you. What happened between your mother and my husband was a long time ago, and it was not your fault."

"Was my father a good husband? A good father?"

Rebecca considered her answer with care. "Yes, both. But there was always this sadness deep inside him. I think it's because he couldn't be the kind of father to you that he wanted to be. I've gathered a few things together for you. If you'll wait a minute, I'll get them."

Rebecca went to the bedroom and then rejoined them, her arms wrapped around the large box filled with pictures and mementos of Jim and the kids that she had prepared for Jin.

"Jeffrey said Jim sent money to your mother. Did you know that?"

Jin nodded. "Yes. And he visit a time or two. But I young. Not really know him."

Rebecca handed him the box. "Well, maybe this'll help you get to know him. I never knew your mother, but I did know my husband. And I'll tell you this much; I believe he loved you. Even though he couldn't show it or tell you himself, I'm sure he loved you as best he could. I know he did as much as he was able to take care of you. He was that kind of man. An honorable man who lived up to his responsibility as a father."

Taking a deep breath, she determined to be obedient to what God had shown her when she chose things to pack in the box. "As a Christian, I am commanded to look after orphans. You're not only an orphan, but my husband's child, and brother to my children. So, I'll honor my husband and my Lord by welcoming you into my family and by providing for you as Jim, and God, would expect of me."

She handed him an envelope with a savings account passbook in it. "I've opened you a bank account with the equivalent of each of my children's trust funds left to them by their father. I'm sure he would have wanted you to have the same."

Jin's eyes widened when he looked at the amount. "This fortune! You sure?"

"Jim was a very wise investor. He set up accounts for me and the children early and added to them regularly. This is what was left in mine. We'll go to the bank tomorrow and make sure everything's legal and available when you need or want it."

She paused.

"And Jin, you can always transfer from one college to another, even out of state. There's nothing wrong with transferring your schooling to, say, New York, so you can be near family."

Jin blinked. His expression was confused, wondrous, emotional. He struggled for a moment before speaking. "But what will you do? How will you live?"

Rebecca smiled at his concern. "My grandmother's estate is more than adequate for providing for me. And I've been promised that the Bed & Breakfast Ray and I are opening will be a huge success."

The joy of obedience filled her heart to overflowing, manifesting itself in irrepressible laughter. "Besides that, my new husband is a very wealthy man."

She regarded Ray with a grin then focused once more on Jin. "But you think about everything, OK?"

The October sky shone clear and crisp. The air was ripe with the scent of grapes. Rebecca stood in the doorway of the cottage and watched her husband help the pickers harvest the sweet, luscious fruit. After the wedding and subsequent trip to Washington and back, she and Ray settled quickly into a state of bliss unlike anything she'd ever dreamed. Nights of passion overflowed into days filled with love and laughter.

Their belated honeymoon in France had been both celebration and reunion when Jeffrey joined them. He and Rebecca told Debbie of Jin's existence and though initially upset, unlike her volatile brother, she accepted the fact that she had another brother with poise, and grace.

That time of love, laughter and familial bonding was surpassed only by the blessings to come. Due to open in the spring, *Becca's Place*'s first, unofficial guests would be Jeff and Debbie when they came home for the Christmas holidays.

Jin had called often and would be joining them for the holidays and beyond, as he completed his semester and transferred to a New York college.

The baby in her womb stirred. Rebecca's heart thrilled. The gift of promise heralded by the holiday season was even greater this year since she was due to deliver her and Ray's baby—a daughter whom they'd decided to name Breanna Mae—on or about Christmas day.

Ray looked up from his chore to see his wife standing in the doorway of their cottage. A wealth of emotions filled his soul, poured through his veins. Never in his wildest dreams had he imagined life could be this wonderful and love so sweet. Nor had he dreamed that one woman could become so much a part of him. His heart. His life. The very breath he took.

Excusing himself he strode toward her, allowing everything he felt to come to the surface, show in his face, and be revealed in his walk.

He didn't care if the rough-and-tough harvesters thought of him as hen-pecked or a sentimental fool. He loved her and was grateful and humbled that she loved him in return. And though her love was blessing enough, he had gained an entire family, which he treasured dearly. And very soon there will be another to adore, honor and cherish. A child. His daughter. Flesh of his flesh and heart of his heart.

He sent up a silent prayer of gratitude as he had every day since they discovered Rebecca was expecting. Despite the fears and concerns, she and the baby remained healthy throughout the pregnancy.

Reaching the bottom step that led to the doorway where

Rebecca waited, Ray hesitated. His gaze locked with hers in a tender embrace. No words were necessary as he closed the distance between them, lifted his hand to cup her cheek, and touched his lips to hers.

The End

If you enjoyed **The Inheritance**, you might also like **Kyleigh's Cowboy**... She's attempting to start a new life. He's roamed for more than a decade. Can they let go of the past and grab hold of the future? Get it Today by Clicking the QR Code Below!

Dear Readers,

For those of you who've followed me and read some of my books, I pray that you've enjoyed ***The Inheritance*** as much or even more that the other's you've read. For new fans, welcome to my world!

Out of all of my books, this was one of the easiest and most fun to write**. *The Inheritance*** is about the chance we all long for...the chance to start over. And, though Rebecca has her share of challenges, she shows that through the love of God and a relationship with Him through the Lord Jesus Christ, and by the power of the Holy Spirit, we can start anew. After all, God is a god of second chances. Of new beginnings. And His mercies are new every morning.

If you don't know Him already, I pray you, too, will pursue a relationship with the Lord Jesus. And, if you do, that you will call upon Him in your time of trouble, for He will hear and answer.

As always, may God bless and keep you and yours in the palm of His mighty hand!

Pamela S Thibodeaux, ***"Inspirational with an Edge!"*** ™

About the Author

Pamela S. Thibodeaux grew up in the town of Iowa, Louisiana. She is the mother of four (two by blood and two by marriage) and a grandmother. A deeply committed Christian, Pamela firmly believes in God and His promises.

"God is very real to me, and I feel people today need and want to hear more of His truths wherever they can glean them. People are hungry for practical (and real) Christian values, not some 'holier-than-thou' dictates which are impossible to believe and difficult to live up to," Pamela says.

"I do my best to encourage readers to develop a personal relationship with God. The deepest desire of my heart is to glorify God and to get His message of faith, trust, and forgiveness to a hurting world."

Email Pamela at: pam@pamelathibodeaux.com
Visit her website: http://www.pamelathibodeaux.com
Or blog: http://pamswildroseblog.blogspot.com

Sign up to receive ***Pam's Newsletter*** and get a FREE short story.

Also: be sure to follow Pam on Social Media: FaceBook, Twitter @psthib, Instagram, Pinterest, GoodReads, and BookBub.

Other Titles by Pamela S. Thibodeaux

Kyleigh's Cowboy
She's attempting to start a new life. He's roamed for more than a decade. Can they let go of the past and grab hold of the future?

Seven years after the death of her husband, Kyleigh Winters turned their old vacation home into a brand new guest ranch. Not willing to join the ranks of lonely women trolling the bars or online in search of a man, Kyleigh is sure if God wishes her to have another husband, He'll send the perfect someone in His own time. But will she be open to the possibility of new love when He does?

Searching for a place that calls to his soul, Lance Stevens has been a roaming cowboy for ten years since retiring from the Marines. He finds that sanctuary the moment he drives through the Silver Star's gate and meeting the lovely owner speaks to more than his soul. Will he open to the healing power of love?

Get this second chance romance novella today and see how love and faith conquers all.

My Heart Weeps
When life takes everything, your world stops. Can a retreat heal the broken lives of two wounded souls?

Melena Rhyker's world shattered the day her husband died. Lost without the man of her dreams, she digs deep to find a path out of her sorrow. Discovering an artistic retreat, she vows to find a reason to carry on and focus her life in a new direction. Can she heal her own heart, and find her new beginning?

Garrett Saunders knows pain. He's spent most of his life hiding from his past. Regrets and lies haunt him, but he longs to leave them behind and embrace his true self. Will Melena's efforts to rebuild her life in the face of such grief encourage him to exorcise his own demons of guilt and shame?

Will two hurting people find peace, wholeness and perhaps love in the heart of Texas?

Get this second chance women's fiction novel today and see how love and faith conquers all.

Keri's Christmas Wish

Controversy and Inconsistencies are thieves of holiday joy for Keri...is there any hope for a happy holiday season?

For as long as she can remember, Keri Jackson has despised the hype and commercialism around Christmas—especially with the controversy over the time of Jesus' birth. Will she get her wish and be free of the angst to truly enjoy Christmas this year?

Jeremy Hinton thinks Keri is a highly intelligent, deeply emotional, and intensely complex woman and he's as fascinated by her aversion to Christmas as he is of the woman herself. A devout Christian at heart, he's studied all of the world's religions and homeopathic healing modalities. But when a rare bacterial infection threatens her life, will all of his faith and training be for naught?

Fans of near death experiences will enjoy this woman's mystical journey into spiritual Truth.

Circles of Fate

When two souls are torn apart by duty, can the hand of God bring them back to a happily ever after?

Late Vietnam War era. Strapped for cash, Todd Jameson flirts with disaster. Caught robbing a liquor store to pay for his dad's funeral and given the choice of jail or signing up for the military, he picks the best of two bad options and joins the army. But just as his fresh start reconnects him with a sense of honor and the friendship of a gracious woman, he's deployed overseas into an unknown destiny.

Sixteen-year-old Shaunna Chatman devotes every breath to caring for her sick mother. Working in a diner to make ends meet, the last thing on her agenda is to fall for a young soldier about to be sent into battle. But when he encourages her not to wait, she reluctantly moves on to wed another who's there to pick up the pieces after she buries her beloved mom.

Thrown into a whirlwind of circumstance, Todd flows in and out of the courageous girl's narrative wondering if their stories will ever fully entwine. And though Shaunna's journey grants her a child even as personal tragedy strikes, her thoughts often turn to the boy who still fills her heart.

Will their paths merge once more to bask in the glory of His love?

Circles of Fate is a deeply woven inspirational women's fiction novel. If you like believable heroes, roads to enlightenment, and tales of inner strength, then you'll adore Pamela S Thibodeaux's romantic saga.

Buy *Circles of Fate* to walk in the light today!

The Visionary

Will the ugly secret haunting the twins keep them from finding true love?

While most visionaries see into the future, Taylor sees

the past. but only as it pertains to her work. Hailed by her peers as "a visionary with an instinct for beauty and an eye for the unique" Taylor is undoubtedly a brilliant architect and gifted designer. But she and twin brother Trevor, share more than a successful business. The two share a childhood wrought with lies and deceit and the kind of abuse that's disturbingly prevalent in today's society.

Can the love of God and the awesome healing power of His grace and mercy free the twins from their past and open their hearts to the good plan and the future He has for their lives?

Love's Overcoming Power

Temptation, Abuse, Grief, and Doubt are plagues common to women all over the world. In John, 16 Jesus said.... In the world you will have tribulation but be of good cheer, for I have overcome the world.

In this Women's Fiction collection comprised of three full-length novels and one novella, Pamela S Thibodeaux shares stories that exemplify the power of God's love to overcome whatever situations life throws at you.

Includes: *The Visionary, Circles of Fate, My Heart Weeps* and *Keri's Christmas Wish.*

The Tempered Series Collection

Start at the beginning and follow these beloved characters throughout the years as love crosses the lines of age and strengthens the bonds of friendship. Contains: *Tempered Hearts, Tempered Dreams, Tempered Fire, Tempered Joy, Lori's Redemption*

Tempered Hearts (book 1 in Tempered series)

An innocent veterinarian. A jaded cowboy. Will they get burned under a Texas sun or find the heat that leads to happily ever after?

Craig Harris has sworn off relationships. He's been burned and betrayed too many times to count. But when he crosses paths with the hot-tempered veterinarian his grandfather hired for the summer will he let go of hurt and mistrust to find the true love he's always longed for?

Tamera Collins is in no mood to put up with an arrogant jerk cowboy even if he is her boss. Grieving too-recent losses leaves her wary of the strong attraction between her and Craig. Can she overcome heartache and shattered faith and open up to their blossoming love?

Tempered Hearts is the first installment of a 5-part family saga where love crosses the lines of age and strengthens the bonds of friendship, and where faith is passed down through the generations proving the sovereignty of God.

Tempered Dreams (book 2 in Tempered Series)

He took an oath to preserve life. Can he stick to it when the woman he loves is in jeopardy?

Dr. Scott Hensley (introduced in Tempered Hearts) has built a wall around his heart since the death of his wife and parents. Katrina Simmons is recovering from scars inflicted on her as a battered wife. Can dreams be renewed and faith strengthened? Can they find joy and peace in God's love and in love for one another?

Tempered Fire (book 3 in Tempered Series)

The daughter of a wealthy rancher... A nobody from

nowhere with nothing…Will their love survive?
Amber Harris is a good girl on the brink of womanhood. Stanley Morrison is a young man at the start of his life. For each other, they have always felt the fireworks that two people in love should feel. But the questions about his past, his pride, and Amber's father might be the end of what could be a strong relationship. As the two try to protect their budding romance, some unlikely but powerful forces conspire to keep them apart. Will they survive the wishes of everyone around them with their relationship intact?

Tempered Joy (book 4 in Tempered series)
He's an 'all around' cowboy. She thinks rodeo cowboys have rocks for brains and a death wish for a soul.

All around rodeo cowboy and heir to the Rockin' H Ranch, Ace Harris is determined not to fall in love. He's only loved one woman in his life, his mother, and no one can even come close to filling her boots. Lexie Morgan thinks rodeo cowboys have rocks for brains and a death wish for a soul. A broken childhood and the death of her father and best friend leave her doubting and questioning God (despite her years of religious upbringing) and afraid of love. Can two young people who clash from the onset learn to trust in the healing power of God and find love and happiness amidst tragedy and grief?

Tempered Truth (book 5 in the Tempered Series)
Will the truth set them free, or will it destroy a lifelong friendship?

Fate declared them neighbors. Scandal insisted they were brothers. The fact that they looked enough alike to be twins only added fuel to the rumors flying about their parentage.

For fifty-plus years Craig Harris and Scott Hensley have enjoyed a bond nothing can sever.

Not the insinuations that they share the same father.

Not the years of strife and grief and heartache.

Not even death.

Will the truth set them free, or will it destroy the friendship that has lasted a lifetime?

Lori's Redemption (spin-off of Tempered Fire)

Can a notorious bad girl find redemption & win the cowboy preacher's heart?

Lori Strickland (introduced in *Tempered Fire*) has always been known as her father's "wild child" with no desire to change until she meets ex-bull-rider-turned-preacher, Rafe Judson. Her attempts to change her wanton ways come to naught until she realizes redemption only comes with true repentance. Can she find redemption and win the heart of the cowboy preacher?

Love is a Rose (devotional)

Can God use a secular song to speak to someone and touch their heart?

Music is the magical entry into the spirit world, the golden gate into the Kingdom of God. But we mustn't be of the mindset that God only uses Christian music to reach out and touch our mind, heart, and spirit. God uses any and ***every*** means available to speak to His children.

Our job is to be open and receptive.

In this devotional, Pamela S Thibodeaux shares how God opened her spirit to a deeper understanding of the abundance of His grace and mercy through the words of the song, The Rose sung by Country & Western artist Conway Twitty.

Pamela offers Seeds to Ponder and a prayer as she parallels the love of God and the Christian life to each verse of the song.

Praise for Pamela S. Thibodeaux

This book was so beautifully written, that it literally made me cry. The hero and heroine were sympathetic yet flawed and I fell instantly in love with them. Wonderful Christian Cowboy Romance! ~ T.P. Warren Amazon Reader on ***Kyleigh's Cowboy***

"Pamela Thibodeaux uses her masterful story writing art to create a powerful story of how God heals a woman's heart —broken by grief— through recovery, love and triumph." ~ CBA Best-Selling Author DiAnn Mills on ***My Heart Weeps***.

"Loved this book. Wish everyone could read this. Definitely puts all holidays in perspective. If we remember the reason for the holidays then we must put God first.......always. I will certainly recommend this book. Great stuff keep up the great writing." ~ (Amazon) Review of ***Keri's Christmas Wish*** by Reba

"Oh, the passion, faith and just LIFE that flows through this book...powerful writing indeed!" ~ Review of ***Circles of Fate*** by Deena Peterson, Book Reviewer @ A Peek at my Bookshelf and Just One More

"Thibodeaux leads the reader through from the first page to the last without once relinquishing control. She hooks them, holds them, and keeps them enthralled until the last line." ~ Review of ***The Visionary*** by Delia Latham,

author of the "Solomon's Gate" series

*"If you have ever considered Christian fiction bland, then check out the **Tempered Series.** It will be well worth your time."* ~ Amanda Killgore for Huntress Reviews

*"**Lori's Redemption** is fast paced, lots of action, gripping storyline... I loved it. It's gone straight back into my TBR pile."* ~ Clare Revell author of the "Monday's Child" series

"Through Pamela's blessed ability to find God everywhere, even in secular song lyrics, she has written devotions guaranteed to touch the heart and remind the reader of our True Love, the Rose of Sharon." ~ Endorsement for **Love is a Rose** by Linda Yezak, Author, Editor Triple Edge Critique Service

Once Again, Thank You.....

I pray you've been blessed as I have by your purchase of this book. If you've enjoyed **The Inheritance,** please write a positive review, and post it at online retailers and websites where readers gather and/or your social media platforms (FaceBook, Good Reads, BookBub, Twitter, etc).

Sign up to receive my **Newsletter** and get a FREE short story.

Temperance
Publishing